# ZOMBIE SQUAD

## Bad to the Bone

### Decomposed by R. W. Zander

# SCHOLASTIC INC.

NEW YORK  TORONTO  LONDON  AUCKLAND  SYDNEY
MEXICO CITY  NEW DELHI  HONG KONG  BUENOS AIRES

ISBN 0-439-39870-3

12 11 10 9 8 7 6 5 4 3 2 1                    4 5 6 7 8 9/0

Printed in the U.S.A.                                      40

First printing, January 2004

# CHAPTER ONE

I stared up at the movie screen, my palms sweating. Time was running out. The movie was starting, and Tommy wasn't back with the popcorn.

When you've coughed up your money at the box office, there is nothing worse than watching a movie without popcorn. I should know. I've seen every scary movie that's played within twenty miles of this town. That includes the multiplex at the mall. We're talking ten theaters.

I rubbed my hands on my jeans and shifted around in my seat. Where was Tommy? Light bounced over the faces of a dozen or so kids. The ten guys in the back row were sharing three big buckets of popcorn. Turning back, I tried to ignore the smell of butter and the jiggle of candy boxes.

Across the aisle, Hayley Frazier and Denise Berry giggled. What was so funny? I focused on the screen. Giant machines slammed down, stamping out a line of wristwatches in a factory. Funny? Not really.

That was the problem with an after-school matinee. Too many kids. Most kids don't take horror seriously. Though Hayley does have a nice smile.

Me, I take my horror and sci-fi to heart. It started when I saw the first *Men in Black*. Kids kept telling me I looked like Will Smith, which I do. We're both skinny, with dark brown skin and awesome smiles. So I started dressing like those alien investigators. Black pants and a white shirt are my thing now. With a skinny black tie.

And suddenly — *wham!* — I became an agent. I tracked down weird stuff. I made notes about every movie I saw. Then I started collecting things. Horror trading cards, comics, video games, printouts from Web sites. Now it's all stuck together in a big blue notebook my friends call the Freaky Files. The Files are getting too big to carry around, but that's okay. I've got it all in my head.

Yeah, it started as a hobby. But it was put to use when zombies invaded my neighborhood. What, you ask, is a zombie? Take it from the Files.

Freaky Files Entry: Zombie — a walking, talking

dead person. For some reason, when this guy died, he didn't go on to the next place. He got stuck as a rotting corpse. Totally rotten. We're talking peeled-off skin and moldy green teeth. And you thought your mom was joking about brushing three times a day.

Find it hard to believe? Hey, I just take notes on freaky things. I've always been into how weird things happen. Like UFO landings. Or the spuds who hatch from breakfast cereal bowls when kids pour on the milk. Or the mud men who rise from the burning core of the earth. When I started watching zombie movies, I had no idea a bunch of the walking dead would walk right into my best friend's backyard.

I was so mad I hadn't been there that first night. My bud Zack Margolis had gone alone to the graveyard. Kind of crazy, I know, but two of the baddest bullies in town had dared him. And when Parker Tolan and Rick Samuels point the finger at you, well, you squirm.

Anyway, Zack went to the graveyard to trace an old tombstone — so he could prove he'd been there. And while he was working on the tracing, a corpse shot out of a grave.

I know, it sounds scary awesome, until you see one of the zombies yourself. One look at their rotting skin and chalky bones, and it's not so awesome.

Anyway, Zack flew out of the cemetery on his bike. A bunch of zombies followed him home and dug their way into the tunnels under his house. Ever since then, they've kept Zack, our friend Amber, and me on our toes. We've been trying to protect the world from the creepiest of the creepy.

Sort of like the agents in *Men in Black II*. I checked across the aisle. I think Hayley was watching me. But she just flicked her baby dreads over her shoulder and poured some candy into Denise's hands. It made a clattering noise, like the bones of the dead. Whew, I was beginning to think "zombie" even when they weren't around.

"Hey, look what I got!" Tommy scooted into the row. He was shaking a box of Goobers. More rattling.

I took the popcorn from him. "Where's my soda?"

Tommy sank down two chairs away from me and tugged his sweater over his stomach. "I got candy instead. Who needs soda when you can drink water for free?"

"But I gave you money for —"

"Ease up, Kyle," Tommy said. "Have a Goober." He held the box out to me, but I shook my head. "Besides, soda will rot your teeth."

I wanted to tell him that he didn't know the first thing about tooth rot. Once you've stared into the gaping mouth of a zombie, a simple cavity looks attractive. But Tommy wasn't in on the sitch. He was your basic outsider. Not a bad dude, but clueless. Tommy Hernandez was the kid who flattened the back of your sneaker and stabbed you in the arm with his pencil without even realizing it. My other friends didn't like to be around him.

No, Tommy didn't know about the zombies, and he didn't understand the value of my Freaky Files. I kept watch over the zombies with Zack and Amber, who would have come to this movie with me if they weren't trying out for basketball. They're my best friends. Tommy is a friend, too, but he's work. He always pushes just a little too hard, you know?

"I met this girl in the lobby," Tommy said. "What a crack-up. She's wearing this costume with feathers. All Native American."

Pet peeve: when people talk through movies. Maybe I could shut him up by catching him up on the action? "You missed the setup. This bad dude broke into the watch factory. He planted cyber-chips in the watches. See that tiny thing floating through the air?" I asked, nodding at the screen.

"There was another guy in costume, too. Some party or something," Tommy went on.

I kept my eyes on the screen. "And now . . . see those microchips?" I continued. "They come out of the watches and latch onto people. I'll bet that chip's going up the bus driver's nose."

"I think she likes me," Tommy said.

"Shh!" Denise glared at us.

*It wasn't me!* I wanted to blurt out. *I never talk through movies.* I swallowed a tough kernel of popcorn, wishing I had my soda. Maybe coming here with Tommy wasn't such a great idea.

*Watch the movie,* I told myself as Tommy reached for a fistful of popcorn. I tried to focus on the chip that took control of the bus driver. I wanted to see how this would play out. After all, I'm the master of all things freaky.

But now people were moving into the row behind us, bumping my seat.

"I just wanted some of that corn," a girl's voice said. "I do enjoy its yellow hue."

"I invented popcorn," a man said. "You know,

it's a matter of the heat moving the molecules of the —"

"You did *not* invent it," the girl said. "My people grew it from the land for —"

"Shhh!" Denise sputtered.

"Really," I said over my shoulder. "Quiet." The guy was a grown-up. He should know better.

"I'm just saying that we grew popping corn from the earth," the girl whispered loudly. "You were not the first to —"

"Quiet!" I repeated, getting mad. "Some of us are trying to watch."

Across the aisle, Hayley looked at me with approval. I touched my tie, wondering if she was into me.

Behind me there was shuffling, but no more talk. I squinted at the screen as a chip landed on a small dog. But now there was a flurry of motion next to Tommy. I glanced over as a Native American girl sank into the seat beside him.

"May I have some of your corn?" she asked.

"Sure." He fumbled in my direction, his eyes on her.

*Oh, great,* I thought, handing over the bucket. Now the two of them would talk endlessly. This movie was going to be a bust.

Tommy slapped my elbow and mouthed: "The girl from the lobby." As if he'd just won a trip to Space Camp.

Clenching my teeth, I leaned forward to see around Tommy. Her face was turned away, but her dark hair was straight and shiny. And really long. It's a wonder she didn't sit on it. Tommy was holding the bucket as she reached in. Something about her hand caught my eye. Maybe it was the leathery layers of peeling skin. Maybe it was the way her bony fingertips fumbled with the popcorn.

Bony fingers? I pressed my lips together, biting back a groan. My stomach did a free fall.

Her nails were so long they curved back toward her palm. Weird nails. Worse than those fakes the school secretary wears.

I followed the red lines down her arm. Was that some kind of tribal paint — or bloody gashes? Her skin was worn away so that I could see the round knob of her wrist bone.

That hand . . . it was definitely dead.

Tommy's new crush was a zombie.

# CHAPTER TWO

There is nothing like seeing a bony hand rake through your popcorn bucket. It definitely kills the appetite. Or maybe I was freaked by the realization that there were new zombies in town. Amber had thought she'd seen a few ghouls arriving at the Paxituckett train station, but I had hoped she was wrong.

I must have been staring, because Tommy grinned at me, proud of his catch. Okay, it was a little sad. How was I going to tell Tommy that the first girl who'd ever rapped with him had been dead for a few hundred years?

"I am grateful to you," the girl zombie told Tommy. She pushed the popcorn into her mouth and lowered her hand.

That's when I saw her face — all bone. Round cheekbones, square chin, and a hollow triangle of a nose. A leather band held her beautiful hair on her skull like a wig. How could Tommy look at her and not cringe?

"Great costume!" Tommy told her. "Really, it's awesome. Where did you —"

"Shhh!" Denise hissed from across the aisle. Both she and Hayley were staring at us. Hey, it's not every day you see a dead girl hanging out at the movies.

I wondered what Denise and Hayley were thinking. With any luck, everyone would think the zombies were in costume.

Ever since the zombies came, Zack, Amber and I had tried hard to keep them hidden. Mostly from kids like Tommy, who were big mouths. Tommy just could not keep a secret.

It was time for damage control. I had to get Tommy out of here — fast. "You know," I said, trying to play it cool. "This movie stinks like yesterday's lunch. Why don't we go?"

Tommy's eyes were suspicious. "Back off. I was just asking her — hey, what's your name?"

"I am called Red Sky," the zombie girl answered as she dug into the popcorn again. For a dead girl, she had a healthy appetite.

"Red Sky was just going to tell me about her costume," Tommy said.

He wasn't budging. I was talking to a mountain of resistance. "The thing is," I said, "you can't talk here. Why don't we head outside and —"

"Kyle Jackson . . . shut up!" Hayley called across the aisle. I shrugged an apology, hating that schoolteacher look in her eyes.

I slapped Tommy's knee. "See? Let's go."

"Go yourself," he said. "I was just asking Sky about her costume."

"Do you fancy it?" Sky pressed her fingers over the brown feathers sewn onto her dress. She wore a long necklace that looked like it was made of seashells. "I collected them myself. Eagle feathers."

"No, no," Tommy said quickly, "I was talking about that cool skin on your arms. It looks like your flesh is splitting open! And your face. Did you glue that fake bone stuff on? Or is it paint? No, wait, it's a mask, right?"

She laughed. "You speak with a lightning tongue!"

"Yeah, Tommy's always been a talker," I said quickly. I slid forward in my seat, trying to get Tommy's attention. "Look, man, the girl has a talent for rubber masks and glue. But this is not a chat room. And if you guys keep yakking, the manager is going to ban us forever."

11

*Pow! Pow!* There was a banging noise at the front of the theater. Everyone turned toward the exit door, where someone was trying to get in. That couldn't be good. Time to go.

I stood up and hunched over Tommy. "Why don't we rent a video? We can watch *Temple of Gloom* again," I said lamely.

"Don't think so." Tommy shoved a finger into my chest. "Sit down, Kyle. Don't ruin this."

A scream rang out. It was in the soundtrack, but no one seemed to be watching the movie anymore. Everyone was looking toward the exit door as it slammed open. A ray of sunlight lit the dark figure who marched inside and stormed right up to the screen. As the dude swung around, I recognized the ax sticking out of his back.

Oh, great! It was Lassiter.

Freaky Files Entry: Isaac Lassiter — one wicked zombie dude. The worst. He used to be a lumberjack. Now he has an ax stuck in his back. Definitely dangerous.

He wheeled around in front of the screen. In the light of the projector, his one eye glowed red in his skull. "Out of here! I order you out of here!" Lassiter shouted.

"Eeeeww!" the girls across the aisle screeched. Hayley hugged herself, bouncing in her seat. Denise stamped her feet, as if she couldn't contain her fear. But it was fake fear. They thought this was a big, scary joke.

Yeah, right. They had no idea. I flopped back down in my seat. No reason to call attention to myself if I wasn't going to make a quick exit.

"Criminy," muttered the man behind me. For the first time I turned and shot him a look. Gray hair hung like limp yarn around his tattered ears. Spectacles pinched the peeling skin at the bridge of his nose. He wrapped his white lab coat tighter, as if he could shrink away inside it. But no coat could hide the scabby skin of his rotting neck. Another zombie. "My dear Sky, I told you he wouldn't like us coming here," he said to the zombie girl. "Did I not?"

"Why should he command us?" the girl asked. "He does not move the moon and stars."

I was glad to hear she didn't like Lassiter, either.

Lassiter lifted his bony hand to shield his single eye from the light of the projector. "Where are you?" he called. He was moving slowly, as if sniffing out a rat.

"Hey, get out of the way!" some kid yelled from the back.

Lassiter hissed at the kid as he plodded up the aisle. "Hiding when there are many tasks to be done? We must set to work if we're going to seize the power."

"Seize the power?" Tommy grinned. "Sounds like that infomercial guy on TV. Next thing, he's going to sell us night-glo toothbrushes. Or *Disco Dance Sounds of the Seventies*."

And Mom says *I* watch too much TV. "You know," I muttered to Tommy, "if we complain to the manager, we can get our money back." It was bait. I'd never known Tommy to pass up a chance for cash.

The zombie girl was suddenly on her brittle feet, gasping. I could smell her fear . . . or was that rotting bones? She dashed up the aisle toward the back of the theater. It took me a minute to realize she was dodging Lassiter.

"Hey, don't go!" Tommy twisted around in his seat. "He'll be out of the way in a second, and we can watch the movie."

The weasely zombie in the white coat followed Red Sky. He scuttled out like a roach escaping bug spray. I realized they were afraid of Lassiter. Were they under a spell or something?

Lassiter spotted them and started moving faster. "You dare to flee?" he growled. "Ducking out of work to sit in the dark!"

"Works for me," Tommy said proudly.

That caught Lassiter's attention. He paused in the middle of the aisle, his red eye darting toward Tommy.

Cold fear trickled down my spine. *Tommy's big mouth strikes again,* I thought, sinking down in my seat . . .

Too late. The zombie was onto me.

"You . . ." Lassiter marched into the row in front of me. His bulk blocked my view. His grotesque face loomed before me. Most of his skin was gone, leaving only a chalky skull. No nose, no hair, and not many teeth.

My heart pounded against my ribs like bongo drums. What did Lassiter want with me?

Tommy was looking back and forth as if following a Ping-Pong match. "You guys know each other?" He took in Lassiter's worn woolen coat, his boots, the ax. "I definitely need one of those for Halloween," Tommy said, pointing at the dangling ax. "That would keep my math teacher

15

off my back for a while." He nudged me. "Get it? Off my back?"

I forced myself to smile. I didn't want Tommy to know how much trouble we were in. He couldn't find out that Lassiter was for real.

"I have a message for you," Lassiter rasped at me. He dragged out the word *you* as if it were glue in his decayed mouth.

I ran a hand over my short 'fro. How I wanted to morph into goo and slide out of there. But I couldn't let Lassiter smell my fear.

The zombie growled, "You and your friends —"

"Hey . . . wait. I'm getting this!" Tommy interrupted. "You're Sky's dad, right? Oh, man." He waved wildly, as if there were a foul on the play. "No big deal. It's just that . . . Whoa! It took me a while to put it together! What, are you guys going to a costume party?"

As Lassiter swung toward Tommy, a voice called from across the aisle. "Cut it out!" said Denise. The girls were getting ticked.

"Yeah!" one of the guys in the back cheered.

This was not good. I squeezed the armrest, wishing I could press a LAUNCH button and eject through the roof.

Lassiter rose up in anger, but Tommy wasn't scared. He didn't even seem to notice.

"Are you visiting?" Tommy went on. "I don't think I've seen Sky at school. We go to Paxituckett Middle School."

"Silence, fool!" The zombie lifted his hand and thrust it toward Tommy's face. Lassiter's curled, gray nails were like claws.

"Hey, mister! Back off, will ya?" Tommy said, leaning back. "Don't you know it's rude to point? You're beginning to creep me out."

Lassiter's single eye bulged red as he focused on Tommy.

"Wait!" I sputtered. This couldn't be happening. He was going to put a whammy on Tommy!

"That's it!" Hayley shot up. "I'm going to get the manager."

"No!" I yelped, wanting her to stay out of it, wanting to protect her from the zombie.

But it was too late. Lassiter stepped back and lifted his hands.

I covered my hands with my eyes, knowing what was coming. A cold, paralyzing spell.

When I slid my fingers away from my eyes, Lassiter was grinning evilly.

Beside me, Tommy was frozen, one hand in

the air, the other in the popcorn. Hayley stood in the aisle like a statue from the park. I didn't have to turn around to see the other kids in the theater. I knew they were numb, powerless to move.

Lassiter had put the whammy on all the kids!

# CHAPTER THREE

Freaky Files Entry: The whammy — when a zombie looks you in the eye and casts a spell on you. It makes you freeze. Not cold, but locked in place. It tends to numb your brain for a while. After a few minutes it wears off.

How do I know this? Zack's little brother, Tyler, got the whammy. And Lassiter put one on Amber. She says it felt awful.

I turned to Tommy. He didn't seem to mind. But now . . . how was I going to explain this to him? To all the kids in this theater?

"Why did you do that?" I hopped out of my seat and swung my fist through the air.

"Stop, before I cast a spell on you, too," Lassiter said. His bloodshot eye was locked on me. If I moved again, I might get the whammy, too.

I stepped back and touched my skinny tie to remind myself that I was on a mission, like the Men in Black. I was a zombie investigator. And although Lassiter was the baddest zombie dude of them all, I wasn't scared. Zack, Amber, and I had tricked him into thinking we possessed some powers. I could use that . . . just as soon as my knees stopped shaking.

"Um . . . your friends headed out that way," I said, pointing toward the lobby. "Don't take it personally, but I think they were trying to ditch you."

"My minions are foolish," Lassiter said, stepping close. So close I could smell his breath. It was a mix of blue cheese and damp earth. Ew. "But you and your friends are the greater fools. You cannot win, even with your secrets and spells. We will take back what belongs to us. Once we find our human slave, no one can stop us."

"A human slave?" I cocked my head. This was a new one on me. Not that I hadn't seen zombies enslave people in movies. But in real life, the whammy seemed to be their main power over humans. They had the whammy and their super-human strength. We had superior brainpower, healthy teeth, and a much better odor.

I figured he was just making threats. "Oh, right. Next thing you'll tell me that you're going to eat my brain." I sat on the armrest and reached into Tommy's popcorn bucket, trying to look cool.

The zombie stepped even closer, so close I could see something wiggling in a hole on his neck. A worm, I think. "Your brain?" he said, grinning. "It's not worth the effort. We're looking for someone older and wiser. Dread wants a brain of great intellect."

"Dread?" I scoffed. "What's that? Your zombie brain-eater?" I was glad I sounded more confident than I felt. I was quaking in my boots.

"Don't cross me," Lassiter hissed. "I've seen your magic, but we shall soon have something far more powerful. We shall reclaim our world."

"Are you talking about the graveyard?" I asked. The zombies were really ticked off about the way humans had dug up their cemetery home. "Because that's a lost cause. Those old bodies have been moved."

Lassiter rubbed his hands together, his fingers clattering eerily. "Oh, those giant shovels opened a lovely can of worms. They've cleared the way for us."

Actually, they were paving the way for our new middle school. I know . . . weird plan. Like one of the architects stole the script from *Ghoul*

*School*. But at least the builders moved all the graves.

"Look, Lassiter," I said, trying to reason with the dead guy. "Your grave is now on the other side of town. Wouldn't you be a whole lot happier hanging in your moldy old crib?" I tipped my hand toward the rows of seats. "You don't belong here."

His mouth gaped open in a jagged smile. Half of his teeth were missing. The other half were in major need of dental care. "It will be ours. You shall see," he insisted.

Okay, I wanted to pull out a neuralyzer and shrink Lassiter into a capsule the size of a pea. But since this wasn't a movie, I had to settle for restraint.

"Good luck, bud," I said, flicking a kernel of popcorn at him. "You're going to need it."

He snarled like a wolf as the popcorn bounced off his dirty plaid shirt. Then he turned and plodded up the aisle after the other two zombies.

I watched the biggest, baddest zombie walk out of the theater, ax bobbing in his back. Around me, kids were frozen like figures in a wax

**22**

museum. I sank down in my chair and rubbed my face.

That's when I made the promise to myself: I had to get rid of him. Lassiter was going to depart Zombieland with a one-way ticket to the Great Beyond. And I, Kyle Jackson, was going to be his travel agent.

Not that I could do it now. It would take some planning. I would need help from my friends.

I reached over for popcorn. Tommy didn't seem to mind the whammy. But I bet it killed him that he was missing out on all this popcorn.

"Hang onto the popcorn," I told him. As if he had any choice. I needed to update the squad while he was frozen.

I sneaked out to the lobby, flipped open my cell phone, and speed dialed Zack's number. He and Amber needed to know that I'd been up close and personal with the new zombies. And they had to hear Lassiter's threat. This was big news for the Zombie Squad.

"Your story is lame," Tommy told me as we walked home from the movie. "I'm not biting."

"I'm telling you, you dozed off!" I insisted.

"There was no girl in a tribal costume sitting with you."

He snapped his fingers at me. "See? I never said she was wearing a costume. *You* saw her. She was real."

Oh, man, I was slipping. Caught by Tommy Hernandez. "Oh, *that* girl . . ." I backpedaled. "Yeah, she was real. Didn't she say something about a costume party?"

"Tell me something, Kyle," he said. "When you look at me, do you see a big *L* on my forehead?"

"Tommy, man, I don't think you're a loser."

"Then you'd better get real, and fast, because while I was in that time warp, I heard you talking with the ax man. Talking about spells and things."

I looked away, calculating. He'd heard that?

Tommy stopped walking, and I knew he meant business. "Now you're going to tell me what *really* happened."

Time for a face-to-face. I tugged on the cuff of my black jacket. "The thing is, I don't really know. I can only tell you what I've read. Similar things that have happened. Weird stuff."

Tommy nodded. "The Freaky Files. Whoa! So something freaky did happen. I knew it!"

24

"Right," I said, trying to figure out how much I could tell him without stirring up more trouble. Right now I didn't have time to deal with Tommy. I needed to get over to Zack's house to talk things out. His mom had even said I could stay for dinner. Pork chops. Major motivation to lose Tommy. "Let's keep walking. We need to keep going. Moving targets are harder to find."

"Okay, okay." Tommy loped along, looking pleased to be on the inside. "So what just happened to me? Was it some kind of spell?"

"I think so," I said. "I think he put a whammy on you. You felt sort of frozen? You couldn't move?"

Tommy nodded. "Yeah, yeah, that's it. A whammy! Is that in your Freaky Files?"

"It is."

"How do you know this stuff? Who else got whammied?"

"A friend of mine," I said. "The thing is . . ." I paused. Although I knew Tommy would want a story, I couldn't give him every detail. "I knew this guy who went into a graveyard one night. It was a full moon, and —"

"A full moon! Your friend wasn't too smart, was he?"

25

"Somebody dared him. Anyway, he went into the cemetery, and this creature rose from the dirt."

"A monster?" Tommy asked.

"More like a human. But dead. A dead guy. And suddenly, my friend was running out of the cemetery and —"

"His first smart move," Tommy interrupted.

"And the dead guy chased him," I went on. "And suddenly, a bunch of dead people were chasing him all the way home. They dragged themselves through his backyard and tried to get into his house."

"So did he call the cops?" Tommy asked. "The police could arrest them for trying to break in."

"Actually, he didn't," I began. "He —"

"What a bonehead!" Tommy interrupted.

I was getting annoyed. "Could I just tell the story?"

"I'm just saying, that's B and E, breaking and entering."

"Well, he couldn't call the cops, because grown-ups don't see the zombies."

"Zombies?" Tommy's mouth popped open. "I thought we were talking about a bunch of dead guys?"

"Walking dead people, yes," I said. "And his parents couldn't see them, so they couldn't protect him."

Freaky Files Entry: Invisible Zombies — zombies cannot be seen by adults. Why not? Who knows? It's like kids have a special vision that they lose as they get older. Example: Trina Margolis, age 16. Zack's sister cannot see zombies. Proof she is so gone.

"Creepy." Tommy seemed to be soaking up the info. "Who saw the zombies? Someone I know?"

I bit my lower lip. Had I said too much? "I . . . uh . . . read about it online. Or maybe I saw it in a movie."

"You said it was a friend of yours."

I ran a hand over my 'fro, trying to get Tommy off the subject. "Well, whatever. The point is, this kid had an encounter with zombies. And I think that's what happened today, too."

Tommy squinted at me. "Aw, you're lying! You know who it happened to. Tell me!"

"That part doesn't matter! The thing is, the guy figured out how to get rid of the zombies. He came up with a way to help them get out of the zombie world. They were sort of stuck in their bodies."

**27**

"And your friend unstuck them?"

I touched my tie, hesitating. If I spoke the words, I would never be able to take them back. This was really what the Zombie Squad was all about, and I worried about letting Tommy in.

"Come on, Kyle." Tommy nudged me with his elbow. "Don't hold back on me now, bud."

I sucked in my breath, then spilled out the truth. "He figured out how to help them move on to the next dimension."

"Cool! Do I know him?" Tommy asked, veering off the subject again. "Your friend. Does he go to our school?"

I felt my nerves straining. "Don't you want to know how you get rid of the zombies?"

Tommy shrugged. "Not really. I liked Sky."

"But she's a zombie! You can't like a zombie."

"Didn't your friend like Sky?"

"Zack never met Sky," I said.

Tommy's face brightened. "Zack? Zack Margolis? This happened to Marshmallow Margolis?"

A sinking feeling came over me. "I didn't say that," I said. Nice fake, Jackson. I was a failed superagent. I might as well bring Tommy to Zack's house and introduce him to Penelope, the old zombie lady who was driving Zack crazy these days.

"Okay, if it wasn't Zack Margolis, who was it?" Tommy said, giving me an out.

Catching the sign over Mel's Butcher Shop, I said, "It was Zack Butcher. I saw it on a TV show."

"I thought you read about him online?" Tommy's said.

Right then and there I gained a new respect for this kid. He was a lot sharper than I'd realized. "Let's get off who it is and get back to the fact that, yes, you met a zombie today. You definitely had a Freaky File encounter. And you survived, Tommy. You should be proud, man."

Tommy nodded. "Yeah, it was freaky, wasn't it?" He grinned. "Just what I was thinking. I'm sort of a hero. And you know what? I wasn't scared at all!" He tucked his thumbs into the pockets of his jeans. "Which is why I think this could be really big for me." He laughed. "Did I say big? I meant huge. Humongous!"

Now I was confused. "Say what?"

"The local news stations will lap this up. Me, you, and the zombies!"

I shook my head, but Tommy kept right on

going. "Forget local. This will be national. They'll probably fly us to Philadelphia. Maybe even New York. There'll be talk shows. And people will want to meet the zombies and the zombie tamer." He punched me in the shoulder. A friendly jolt, but it nearly socked the life out of me. Or maybe it was his big plans that sucked the air out of my lungs.

"You can't do that," I said. "You can't take the zombies on TV."

"Oh, yeah?" he said challengingly. "Watch me."

As we reached the edge of town and passed the high school, Tommy went on about talk shows and movies and zombie dolls. Now I remembered why I had formed the Zombie Squad with Zack and Amber. My friends and I wanted to get the zombies out of our neighborhood. But that didn't mean sending them to Hollywood or New York was the answer. These walking corpses used to be people. They weren't fake monsters to put into a freak show.

That's when I remembered the glitch in Tommy's plan. "You can't put the zombies on TV," I told him suddenly. "Well, you *can*. But most of America won't see them. Remember what I said? They're invisible to adults."

Tommy smacked his chubby cheek. "Oh, crud. Are you sure?"

"Positive." I watched him take in that info. You could almost see the wheels turning in his head as he tried to put another spin on it.

"Okay, it's a setback. But I'll think of something," he said. "There's got to be a way around it."

I didn't think so. But I was tired of trying to talk Tommy out of things. I let him mull it all over as we walked the three blocks to my house. I was glad to see the old mailbox with the eagle and the little pumpkins Mom had lined up on the front porch. There was a strange car parked in the driveway. A red Cadillac.

"Hey, who does the Caddie belong to?" Tommy asked. He knows cars. His dad owns a dealership in town.

I shrugged as I backed across the lawn. "Maybe a friend of Mom's. So I'll talk to you later?"

"What's your hurry? Let's play some video games or something."

"I've . . . got a few things to do," I said, thinking about Mrs. Margolis's pork chops. Friday dinner at my house was usually a do-it-yourself thing, so I knew it would be no problem for me

31

to go to Zack's. Mom has to put in a few hours at the travel agency on Fridays. That leaves Dad and me to head off to Pizza Pizzaz or order in Chinese. And that's when Dad isn't buried with cases. He's a lawyer, and sometimes he works on the computer at home to stay on top of things.

"What's the big rush?" Tommy put his hands on his hips. "What do you have to do on a Friday night?"

"Homework?" I said, knowing it was a lame answer.

"Yeah, right." Tommy just stood there, not budging. I was stuck with him.

"Okay, come on in," I said. Maybe Mom would give me a chore or two to fend off Tommy.

I bounded up the front steps, ran past the pumpkins, and cut around to the side door. Mom stood at the kitchen counter, talking to a woman at the table. A visitor?

"Kyle, honey!" Mom smiled. "Look who's here."

When the woman turned toward me, I felt the blood drain from my face. It couldn't be . . . not today!

"What is it?" Tommy asked, pushing me aside to see for himself. "Is there a zombie in your house?"

# CHAPTER FOUR

**H**ello, Kyle. Come give your gramma a hug." My grandmother lifted her arms and gave me that look. You know, the don't-tell-me-you're-getting-too-old-for-hugs look.

I crossed the kitchen and let Gramma fold her arms around me.

Don't get me wrong. Gramma is okay. It's just that I wasn't expecting her today, and Gramma is regimented, stubborn, and a lot stricter than my parents. She used to be the elementary school principal here in Paxituckett. Although she retired, she still loves correcting grammar and grading kids. Gramma worried that I watched too much TV. She didn't think my interest in all things weird was "healthy." And if she got a look at my diet, she'd probably give me a C minus.

"You're skinny as a twig," Gramma said. What did I tell you about the C minus? "Growing like a weed, I see. Though I do like your suit."

"Oh, wow, hello, Mrs. Jackson," Tommy said, standing tall. "It's good to see you." He could be such a suck-up when he wanted to.

"Hi, Tommy. Come on in and meet Kyle's gramma, Dinah Jackson," Mom said.

"Yes, come over here, young man." Gramma extended her hand. Her thick African bracelets jangled as she shook Tommy's hand. Her chin-length hair was now a little redder than usual, but otherwise she was the same old Gramma Dinah. Big jewelry, cocoa brown skin, and eyes that watched you like a hawk. "And what's this talk of zombies? Were you two off at one of those gruesome movies Kyle favors?"

"It was about computer chips that fly out of watches," I said, before Tommy could blab everything. "Not so gross."

"Gramma decided to spend the weekend with us," Mom said. "She's a special guest at the groundbreaking on Sunday. I told her you'd clean up the den for her."

"Yeah, sure," I said. My Freaky Files were spread out on the table in the den, where Gramma would be staying. I would have to re-think the weekend. She'd be here to monitor my

TV viewing, limit my computer use, and . . . oh, man! Did Gramma get a look at my Files?

"Yeah, I'll clean up right now," I said, with two goals in mind. I wanted to stash away private info. And I knew the task of cleaning up would scare off Tommy.

"Okay, then," Tommy said in that fake polite voice. "I guess I'd better get going. Nice meeting you, Mrs. Jackson."

"Yes, it's a pleasure to meet a boy with manners," Gramma said.

"I'll call you later," Tommy told me. I hoped I wouldn't be here when he did. My mouth was watering for Mrs. Margolis's pork chops, but I had a feeling those plans were slipping through my fingers.

Gramma was here. That meant early bedtimes, lots of fruits and vegetables, and dinner at the dining room table.

Hey, I liked her just fine. But she definitely cramped my style.

"I was just about to call your cell phone, so it's good that you came home," Mom told me as I rushed to the den, straightening up. I stuffed cards and papers into my Freaky Files folder and hugged it to my chest. "Gramma's making sweet potato pie for dinner," Mom continued. "Liz is going to cover for me at work. And Dad will be home in time to join us, too. Isn't that nice? Eating as a family on Friday night."

"Right," I said, stacking some horror DVDs. I had been hoping to eat as part of the Margolis family tonight, but I'd have to call Zack and scratch that. "Is it okay if I go over to Zack's house after dinner?" I asked.

"We'll see," she said. "It's not often we get to spend the evening together."

I wanted to answer: *It's not often that a new batch of zombies invades the neighborhood!* But I knew I was already pushing it, asking to skip out on a family night.

Dinner was torture.

Everyone took their time, like a film in slow motion. Okay, they were happy to be together, and they didn't have a clue about the threat that could be right outside our door. I mean, Zack's just a few blocks away, and not so long ago he had a basement full of zombies. As Mom carved another wedge of sweet potato pie, I turned toward the big bay window. They were out there, somewhere. Lassiter and the girl and the mad scientist zombie.

"More sweet potato pie, Kyle?" Gramma asked. "Come on, child. You're skin and bones."

"No, thanks," I said. "I'm really full." Suddenly, I couldn't handle mushy orange sweet potato pie. It reminded me of the graveyard clay the zombies used to be covered in. But you didn't say that sort of thing to Gramma Dinah. In fact, when she was around, it was dangerous just to think it.

As Dad commented on the salad, Gramma put down her fork and eyed me suspiciously. I knew she couldn't read my thoughts, but that look made me feel like she could.

"Yes," Gramma said, "I've got my eye on you, Kyle. I saw part of your project. Your reports on science-fiction films. Is that still your hobby?"

"I guess so." I shrugged. "But it's changing. I used to do anything for a good scare. Now, I'm more interested in . . ." I was going to say dead people, but I shaved it down to " . . . people."

Gramma took a biscuit from the basket. "Really? Are we talking psychology or history?"

"History." I jiggled one foot under the table.

This was getting a little close for comfort, but I figured it was good to get it out. Sooner or later my parents were going to check some of the Web sites I'd hit on lately. "I've been surfing the Web," I said. "And you can find so much. Family trees. Local history. Civil War battles. Local businesses. Historical societies."

Gramma nearly dropped her biscuit. "Kyle, that's marvelous!"

Dad shot me a smile. "And all this time, I thought you were in your room playing Tetris."

I shrugged. "That, too."

"Well, history is valuable in many ways," Gramma said. "We can learn by the mistakes of others. And it gives our world a context."

*And it can help you send a zombie to another dimension,* I thought. Of course, I couldn't tell Gramma I'd been researching the lives of zombies. But the two zombies who'd vanished from this world made it out because of the history that Zack, Amber, and I had patched together. Along with my infinite knowledge of all things freaky.

Gramma's eyes gleamed with pride. It was as if I'd hit a homer for her team.

I figured it was as good a time as any to duck

out. "Can I be excused now?" I asked. "I'm supposed to go over to Zack's house."

"*May* I be excused," Gramma corrected.

"And I never said you could go," Mom said.

But Gramma threw me a fastball. "It's Friday night, Carol. The boy's got to have some fun."

"All right." Mom nodded.

I tossed my napkin on the table and just barely managed to refrain from letting out a cheer.

"Just one more thing before you go," Gramma said. "I brought a gift for the family. And I imagine that you, Kyle, are the only one who really enjoys tearing through wrapping paper these days. " She pointed to a flat, tall package leaning against the hutch.

"Sure," I said, sizing up the big package. It was too flat to be a big-screen TV, too small to be a foosball table. I tugged off the bow and sank my fingers into the paper.

"Careful, there, Kyle," Gramma warned. "It's glass, and it's been in the family for generations."

I tore down and the paper separated. Peering in, I saw a brown face staring back at me. "It's a mirror," I said.

"The one with the gilded frame?" Dad got up from the table to take a look. "Mama, that's great! I remember when it hung in Gramma Felicia's parlor."

"It's really quite grand," Mom said. From the way she tugged on her ear, I could tell something was wrong. She probably wasn't crazy about the mirror. "Oh, Dinah, are you sure you want to part with it?"

"I wanted you and Marcus to have it," Gramma insisted. "That way it will always stay in the family."

"Cool," I said. "Thanks, Gramma." I looked toward the door. "Can I go now?"

Just then the phone rang and I dashed into the kitchen to answer it. "Hernandez Morgue calling," Tommy said. "You kill 'em, we chill 'em."

"Duh!" I turned away so that no one in the dining room could hear me. "Can you just get off the zombie stuff?"

"That's pretty impossible. I mean, it's totally amazing and totally gross. When do you think they'll appear again? Do they haunt the cinema?"

"Today was the first time I saw them there," I said, realizing Tommy had a good question.

Where *was* Lassiter hanging out? The other zombies had taken over the tunnels in Zack's basement. They liked the cool, damp earth there. Penelope, the old lady zombie, was still there, but Lassiter had run away a few weeks ago. Where did he run to?

"I'm working on this," Tommy went on. "There's got to be a way to do something really big with these zombies. We could be famous."

"Just let it go, okay?" I said, pacing the kitchen.

"No way. And you're my zombie connection, bud. I've been thinking about what happened while I was whammied. You talking with the ax man. That dude seemed to know you."

"I can't help you," I insisted.

"Oh, I think you can," Tommy said. "And you will."

I didn't have time to argue. I told Tommy I had to go, then shouted good-bye before ducking out the kitchen door. I ran the three blocks to Zack's house, then knocked on the back door.

"Hello, Kyle," Zack's mother answered. "They're downstairs as usual." She shook her head. "I never thought we'd get so much use out of the basement when we bought this house."

"Really," I said. If only she knew *who* was living in her basement.

Zack's little brother, Tyler, sat at the kitchen table making figures out of Play-Doh. "Look, Kyle," he said. "I made Penelope!" He held up a purple stick figure with Play-Doh strings of hair.

"That's great, pumpkin," Mrs. Margolis said, turning back to the dishwasher. "Is Penelope a girl at day care?"

"No," Tyler said. "She's the old granny who lives in the basement."

Oh, great! Tyler was talking about the zombies again! We'd told him to keep it a secret. I paused with my hand on the knob of the basement door, wondering what Mrs. Margolis would do.

She laughed. "Is that right? You have a fabulous imagination, Tyler."

"Here I am, squad members," I called down to the basement as the door closed behind me. "Fresh from the most recent Lassiter sighting. And I managed to put Tommy off the trail, but not for long."

"Tommy Hernandez is a total snoop," Amber said as the wooden stairs creaked under my feet. "That kid doesn't know when to back off."

42

"And he lives right across the street," Zack said. "Sometimes I can just feel him watching at the window with little binoculars."

Amber was throwing Velcro balls at a dartboard. Zack sat on the dryer, reading over some papers. I pulled a ball off the board. "How can you sit around tossing balls when we're in deep trouble?"

"We've been in trouble ever since they followed me home from the graveyard," Zack said, running a hand over his close-cut brown hair. "You get used to the constant panic. You get numb."

"Well, I'm here to give you a kick in the butt," I said. "Lassiter is planning something. Something about getting a human slave."

Zack dropped the papers in his lap and slapped his hands over his ears. "No, don't tell me. I was getting used to numb."

Amber tossed a ball for a bull's eye. "And I thought things would be easy once we got rid of Chastity." Chastity was a girl zombie who had tortured Amber. She'd loved all the frilly things Amber hated.

But now Chastity and the zombie Jeremiah were gone. We sort of helped them move into the

**43**

next dimension by solving problems they each had. See, not all the bodies in the old graveyard turned into zombies. It was only a handful who didn't make it to eternal rest. We've figured out that the zombies are stuck here because they have a key issue.

Freaky Files Entry: Key Issue — the hook that snags a dead person. Until this problem is solved, the dead guy can't go on to the place where dead people are supposed to go. It's as if these zombies can never make it to level six of *Time Warp.* They can't score high enough to steer the Sonic Saucer for that final ride.

Zack and Amber and I had just figured out Chastity's key issue — that she put so much value on things. The girl was a regular klepto. Once the problem was really solved, Chastity went *poof!* She was restored to her beautiful self, then she danced off with her ghost parents.

I couldn't wait to send Lassiter on a sonic cruise to never-never land. But Lassiter's key issue was going to be a challenge. The ax man didn't want to go to the next dimension. This dude would fight it all the way.

I climbed up on the dryer beside Zack. He

was intent on reading the photocopies. "What's that?"

"Stuff from the historical society," he said. He pulled a pencil from behind his ear and circled something. "After your call, I headed over there to see if they had anything on Lassiter."

"And you found this?" I asked.

Zack handed me the top page. "The volunteer there helped me find these in the old sheriff's files. I made a copy of any page with Isaac Lassiter's name on it."

I squinted at the paper. OAK COUNTY SHERIFF'S OFFICE, 1846 was written at the top in swirly writing. The bottom part had lists handwritten in script. "Looks like the right time. Whose writing is this?"

"The sheriff's. We made copies from an old ledger that proves Lassiter was in jail," Zack said. "But I haven't been able to find what he did wrong. This handwriting is hard to decipher, and everything is in here. Stolen chickens. Spitting in public. A stray goat that ruined someone's vegetable garden."

"They put a goat in jail?" Amber asked as she went to the board to pull off the Velcro balls.

Amber is the most athletic girl I know. She's a maniac on the soccer field, but off the field she's very low-key. A backward baseball cap covered her head, though a few red curls sprang out under the back.

Zack shrugged. "It looks like the goat's owner got in trouble. Hey, wait. This is it! 'Isaac Lassiter formally charged today. Will stand trial for the cruel and malicious act of murtle.'"

"Murtle?" I leaned over Zack's shoulder and squinted at the paper. "That's not murtle, it's —"

Zack and I said the word at the same time: "Murder!"

# CHAPTER FIVE

**O**h, man — game over. We're in the danger zone now." I slid off the dryer and rubbed my hands together. "I always knew Lassiter was trouble, but I had no idea how bad it was." Fear clenched my stomach. It was as if I were roaring down a roller coaster. I never felt scared by movies or books anymore. Never. But once real danger walks into your life, the fear factor changes.

"Now hold on . . . we don't know that he was guilty yet," Amber said, reading over Zack's shoulder. "Does it say anything about witnesses?"

Zack frowned. "There's something here about evidence — a bag of stolen gold was found in Lassiter's cloak."

"Stolen gold." I swung my arms in a windup and tossed one of the Velcro balls. It landed on a sweater hanging on the line. "Could have been put there to trap him."

"Wait, wait, wait!" Amber pointed to the next

page. "And there were witnesses — two lumber-men. Their names are scratched in here."

"Oh, man." Zack moaned. "Sounds like Lassiter was one bad dude."

"And now he's one bad zombie," I said. This was serious. Like it wasn't bad enough that we had a pack of rotting zombies to deal with. Now we knew one of them was really evil. We would have to be supercareful around this guy. "Was Lassiter found guilty?" I asked.

Zack leafed ahead through the papers. "Let's see. The trial began in April. Two more trial entries. And then . . ." he winced. "He escaped!"

"What?" Amber's jaw dropped. "Lassiter escaped from jail?"

Zack nodded. "A week into the trial, Lassiter's cell was empty. 'Prisoner escaped. Manhunt begun.'"

"So he got away," I said. "Which explains why he wasn't hanged as a murderer."

"But that ax in his back is pretty obvious," Zack said. "Somebody took justice into their own hands."

"Or else he just crossed the wrong person," Amber said. "Lassiter doesn't have a people-pleasing personality."

"That's for sure," I said. "We've got to find out more. I wonder if Penelope knows what he's up to. Where is the zombie queen, anyway?"

"Taking her mud bath," Amber said.

"And we're not going in there." Zack glanced at the door to the tunnels. "Mom's been complaining about all the mud getting tracked through the house. She doesn't know the dirt is from the tunnels. And, let me remind you, we're not supposed to be in there."

The tunnels were built to hide runaway slaves during the days of the Underground Railroad. Zack's parents knew about them when they bought the house, but the door to the tunnels was sealed off.

Until the zombies dug their way in. They liked the mud there. They needed something cool and damp to keep decay away.

Freaky Files Entry: Zombie Mud Bath — the only way to keep dead skin from totally rotting. The zombies need to pack mud around them and rest in it for at least part of the day.

"How about if we invite Penelope to come out?" I suggested. "Maybe she can explain Lassiter's threat about snagging a human."

"Not a bad idea," Amber said. "We really need

**49**

more info on the rude dude. I'd love to send him off before he whammies half of Paxituckett."

"Really!" I said, thinking back to when I saw the ax man in the theaters. "Whatever he's planning, he seems dead serious."

"*Dead* being the operative word?" Amber joked.

I grinned. You gotta love Amber. She never loses her sense of humor. "I'll go wake up Penelope," I said, tugging on the heavy door to the tunnels. "Maybe she can help us."

"Be sure to wipe your feet on the way out," Zack said, tossing a ball at the target.

Freaky Files Entry: Penelope Merriweather — an old woman with a thing for baking. From her scorched dress, she probably died in a fire. She's a disaster in the kitchen. Burns everything, but you got to give the woman credit: She keeps on trying to bake it right.

My high-tops scraped along the hard-packed dirt floor as I stepped inside. I waited a moment for my eyes to adjust to the darkness, then moved ahead. Penelope's favorite sleeping spot was in a short tunnel that dead-ended quickly.

There, near my feet, was her body. She was stretched out on her back, covered in dirt. The imprint of her face was clear beneath the mud coating. Actually, Penelope didn't have much of a face left. Just bone and eyes drooping from the sockets. Flat as fried eggs.

"Penelope," I called. Oops. She was big on formality. "Excuse me, Miss Merriweather? You need to wake up. I mean . . . rise and shine, ma'am. Your presence is requested in the front of the basement."

The mud over her face crumbled. She sat up, and the dirt skittered away. "Oh, how lovely. Is it a tea party, then?"

"Sure," I said, fanning the dust away from my face. "A party without the tea." I offered her my hand, and she rose out of the mud.

"How charming." She brushed off her scorched skirts, straightened her crumpled hat, then linked her arm through mine.

Gross out, I know. Arm in arm with a dead lady. But what could I do? It was the only way to find out about Lassiter.

I was glad when we reached the door to the basement. "After you," I said, trying to mind my manners. Actually, I tried to act like every butler I'd ever seen in a movie. At least they were polite, and Penelope went for that.

She stepped over the threshold and lifted her chin. "Good day," she told Zack and Amber. "Would you be so kind as to find me a chair, young man?"

Zack turned to me and rolled his eyes. I could see he was up to his eyeballs with Penelope. I went to the closet and took out a folding chair. Penelope sat down as if she were sunning herself in the park. She glanced over at Amber, who stared right back.

"A most unfortunate bonnet, my dear," the zombie said.

Amber took off the baseball cap, scratched her curls, then plunked the hat back on. "Works for me," she said.

Penelope folded her bony hands on her lap. "Didn't you say there was tea? I wouldn't mind a few pastries."

"But zombies don't eat," I said. Okay, I'd seen Red Sky munching popcorn in the movies. And Lassiter always had a hungry look in his eyes. But we had gotten past the notion that zombies ate human brains, the way they do in the movie *Dead Ghouls Walking*.

"We don't need food," Penelope said. "But it is such a delight, don't you think? The way your teeth feel when they sink into a fresh-baked cookie?"

She rubbed her hands together, finger bones rattling. "How I'd love to bake some muffins for you children. Or maybe a pie? I used to make a lovely gooseberry tart. My beau Mortimer adored my tarts. Shall we remove ourselves to the kitchen?"

"Not now, we can't," Zack said firmly. "My parents are home, and they're starting to get suspicious. Trina keeps calling me Emeril. Mom thinks I'm the one baking all those burnt cookies and cakes."

"I didn't burn them!" Penelope insisted. "I never burned anything."

Serious denial. Apparently, we'd hit a sore spot for Pyro Granny. "Okay, okay, don't worry, Miss Merriweather," I said. "You'll have a chance to bake plenty more cookies."

"Can we just get to the point here?" Zack asked, pacing nervously.

"Right," I said, turning to the zombie. "Miss Merriweather, we need your help. It's about Lassiter . . . Isaac Lassiter? The guy with the ax in his back?"

"Indeed." Penelope brushed a speck of mud

from her scorched dress. "I never cared for the likes of that one. The scalawag. A scoundrel."

"No argument here," Amber said.

"I should hope not," the zombie said, glaring at Amber.

"Lassiter seems to have some kind of plan," I said. "Did he ever mention it to you?"

Penelope pressed a bare finger against her chinbone. It clicked as she tapped it there. "Oh, he's full of anger, that one. At first it was about defending sacred ground — our homes in the cemetery."

"The old cemetery," Amber said aloud.

The old cemetery that was going to be our school next year. I still couldn't get over that bonehead plan. It wasn't going to be fun, sitting in algebra and wondering whose bones used to lie rotting under your desk.

"All of the graves have been cleared away," Zack said. "They're ready to break ground for the new school."

"Gramma is here for the big ceremony on Sunday," I added. "I wonder if Lassiter is still feeling sentimental about the place?"

"Oh, I'm sure of that. He's a stubborn man," Penelope said. "And alas, there is that troublesome legend about the human leader . . ." Her voice trailed off. "But I'm sure you know it."

"Whoa, whoa, whoa!" Amber held up her hands like a soccer goalie. "What legend?"

Penelope let out a sigh. "Oh, you know! It just whirls around in your bones." Cocking her head to the side, she began to recite:

"When the graves are upturned and the moon
    glows red,
A single human shall lead the dead.
We will hunt, we will scour, till the day we find
The one living human to lead zombiekind."

I felt my jaw drop. What was this, some dire prediction? "Where did you hear that?" I asked.

Miss Merriweather smiled. "Oh, you know. Graveyard gossip."

Zack's face was pale. "What's the rest?" he asked. "The next part of the poem."

Penelope shrugged. "I don't recall, but, indeed, there is more."

"Great," Amber muttered. "Just when you think it's safe to go in the graveyard, you find out there's a legend about zombies snatching a living person to become their fearless leader."

"Oh, it's not nearly so dismal," Penelope insisted. "Wouldn't it be an honor to be chosen?"

Amber and Zack frowned at me, almost as if it were my fault that Penelope was off her rocker.

"Okay," I stood up and reached for Penelope. "Nap time."

"Oh, dear." Penelope pouted. "And just when the discourse was getting so lively."

"But don't you want to get back to your mud nap?" I asked.

She hugged herself for a minute. Her bony fingers made the dry skin on her arms crackle. "Yes, I should return to my toilette. If you'll excuse me?"

I did my butler bow as Penelope turned and walked back into the tunnels. She might be a hazard in the kitchen, but at least she was happy to stay put in the tunnels.

Unlike Lassiter.

"Well, she's just a big dough ball of info." Zack grabbed an old sponge from the sink and swiped at Penelope's mudprints on the floor. "We've sent two zombies to their rest, and now she tells us about this legend. A human leader? Is it me, or is anyone else quivering in their Keds?"

I was scared, all right. But it would only make Zack feel worse if I admitted it. "Don't let her get to you," I said. "Look, Zack. As soon as we get rid of Lassiter, we'll work on sending Penelope off to La La Land. I promise."

Zack stood up and shot the sponge into the sink. "But how are we going to get rid of Lassiter when he doesn't want to go?"

"We'll find a way," Amber said. "We can do this."

"First we have to find him," I said. "Learn more about him. I have a good idea of where he's hiding out."

Zack pressed his hands to his ears. "Don't tell me what I think you're thinking about where to find Lassiter."

I nodded. "The old cemetery. That's gotta be it. And there's no time to lose. We need to go tonight."

"How did I know you'd say that?" Zack moaned. "Tell me there isn't a red moon tonight. . . ."

I shrugged. "What's a red moon, anyway?"

"I can't go tonight," Amber interrupted, checking her watch. "My Dad is picking me up for an overnight in, like . . . twenty minutes ago.

Okay, he's probably already sitting with Mom in the kitchen, worrying over my math grade."

I turned to Zack. "Looks like it's you and me, bud."

"I must be crazy," Zack said. "Like, didn't I learn my lesson about going to graveyards after dark?"

"We'll be together," I said. "Besides, it's not as if we're going to have a face-to-face with the walking dead. We're just going to stake out the place. See what we can find out."

"Yeah," Zack said sadly, "and the first time, I only went for a grave rubbing."

"Don't sweat it," I said with more confidence than I felt. "Think of it as a spy mission. I'll meet you in front of Pizza Pizzaz at eleven."

"I wish I could trade places with you," Amber said. "Dad is okay, but there's nothing like sneaking through the old cemetery after dark."

"Right," Zack said. "We'll save you a few worms and mud cakes, Amber."

The sky was glowing blue, nearly dark as I walked up the front steps. The porch chairs looked like huddled creatures. I half expected a mildewed monster to jump out from behind one of them.

That was dumb, I know. But do you see how the zombie business gets to you?

The side door was open, and the clothesline out back was swaying. I went over to the rail and saw Gramma was in the yard, taking in the laundry. She stood in front of two flowered sheets that waved in the breeze.

"Home just at sunset?" Gramma said, shaking out one of Dad's shirts. "Cutting it close, Kyle Jackson. You remind me of your father."

I shrugged. "Hey, I learned from the best." I leaned over the porch rail. "So what's the deal for Sunday? Are you giving a speech?"

"A short one," she said. "I guess the mayor thought it right to have an old dinosaur at the groundbreaking for the new school."

"You're not that old, Gramma."

"Older and wiser, child."

The wind kicked up. A sheet behind Gramma flapped up, and I noticed something behind it. A dark figure was hiding there.

My heart hammered in my chest as I bounded down the porch stairs. I ran past Gramma to see.

Lassiter lifted the sheet and grinned his evil grin. He was just a few feet behind my gramma. He'd been watching her. Stalking her. Was he trying to hurt her?

"What are you doing here?" I demanded.

He laughed at me.

Gramma thought I was talking to her. "That's a silly question, child," she answered. "Your mother had some phone calls to make, and I volunteered to bring in the clothes." She stepped toward a sheet, just inches from Lassiter! "Nothing like the smell of fresh-hung laundry," she said, pressing her face to the billowing sheet.

"I stopped by because I smelled something, too," Lassiter said. "Do I detect the odor of fear in the air?"

I stepped between him and Gramma and glared at him.

"Oh, brash boy," the zombie rasped. "Do you really think you frighten me? I know you can't do your magic without your little friends."

Man, I wished I could make him go *poof!* right then and there.

He ducked behind the sheet and came out on the other side. "Actually, I wanted to take you up on your challenge. I wanted to make you pay for

**60**

refusing my order today. But when I arrived, I met a pleasant surprise." He sized up Gramma, using a long, twisted gray fingernail as a pointer. "Strong arms. Hardworking. And smart. I heard her inside, giving instructions on one of those fancy machines. Quite smart. Exactly as the legend calls for." He reached out and flicked his dirty nail under her chin. "Dread and I think she'll do just fine."

"Don't touch her!" I said. "Stay away from her!"

"Kyle!" Gramma whirled around. "Have you lost your marbles?"

I rubbed my face, trying to cover the fear and make up an excuse for Gramma. "There was a ladybug," I said quickly. "On the clothespin. You almost smashed her."

"Oh." She turned the clothespin in her hand. "Well, it's gone now."

Lassiter chuckled. "Have you lost your marbles?" he mimicked. "You'd better find your marbles, boy. Go look for your marbles!"

Gramma rubbed her chin on the spot Lassiter had touched. "Look at that. I'm bleeding."

"No!" I said.

"Must have scratched myself." She smiled.

"Calm down, boy. Have you been eating too much chocolate?"

Lassiter laughed. "Oh, that scratch is just the beginning," he said in an icy voice.

I pulled Gramma toward the house. "You'd better get inside," I said. "You're bleeding and . . . and the blood will attract mosquitoes."

"But I'm not finished," Gramma said.

"I'll do the rest," I said, pushing her bulky back toward the porch. "Those mosquitoes are vicious. Killer mosquitoes. I saw them on the Discovery Channel."

Lassiter bounded up the stairs in front of us. The handle of his ax gleamed in the porch light.

I steered Gramma around him.

"Mosquitoes? What's come over you, child?" Gramma said.

"It's called fear," Lassiter said. "Fear of the dead, if he's a smart boy."

Fear was right. My heart was clanging like a marching band.

As I guided Gramma up the last step, Lassiter sidled up beside her. He was so close, he was breathing into her hair.

"Your grandmother is charming," he said. His fingers unfurled. His long, gray nails brushed at a lock of Gramma's red hair. "She's just what we need."

Panic seeped through me as the zombie reached toward Gramma. *He's going to hurt her,* I thought, *and she doesn't even know it!*

# CHAPTER SIX

I smacked Lassiter's hand away. He laughed, but Gramma eyed me suspiciously.

"Big, fat mosquito," I explained. I turned and slapped Lassiter's arm again.

Dust rose from his dirty sleeve, but he didn't seem fazed. "Stupid boy!" he said. "Do you really think you can protect her?"

"Well, thank you for saving me from those killer insects," Gramma said, touching her chin again. "I'm going to put some antiseptic on this." She opened the door and disappeared inside. Safe.

I spun around to scream at Lassiter. He was back on the lawn, sitting on the picnic table. "Stay away from her!" I said, bounding over to the rail. "One step into this house and I'll . . . I'll cast a spell that'll turn you to dust."

He snarled like a wolf, revealing his rotted teeth. "Do you think you can stop me, boyo?"

"I can, and I will!" I shouted, my fists curled

in fury. I ran to the stairs and bounded down. "You don't scare me!" I said, lunging toward the picnic table.

But when I hit the grass, he was gone. I walked under the clothesline. I checked behind the garage. "Come out and face me, you animal."

But there was no answer. Lassiter was gone.

The big wuss.

"He tried to hurt my gramma!" I said into the phone. I was on a three-way call with Amber and Zack. "He's after her. I can tell!"

"Lassiter?" Amber's voice squeaked. "No way! I am so mad I'm missing this! I would have kicked his big, fat zombie butt clear to Pittsburgh."

"Hey, I missed it, too, and I'm only a few blocks away," Zack said. "Kyle, take a breath and spill. Tell us everything."

I did. Amber was in awe. Zack sounded a little shaky.

"You go, Kyle!" Amber said. "I can't believe you actually touched that googly cyclops!"

"Maybe we should forget this cemetery thing," Zack said. "It sounds like he's got your house staked out."

"No! We need to go," I insisted. "I thought about Gramma, but she's staying in, and I told him if he came into the house, I'd cast a huge spell on him."

"And that worked?" Amber sounded impressed. "Maybe we should threaten him more often."

"It'll work for now," I said. "Gramma's okay for tonight. The main thing is, we've got to send Lassiter off to the next dimension soon. Before he can get to Gramma and turn her into a walking zombie."

"Whoa!" Amber said. "Do you really think she's the one? Maybe he's just taunting you, Kyle."

"I wish — but why else would he be in my backyard, scratching my gramma with his claws?"

"This mission is sounding worse and worse to me," Zack said.

"No, no! Remember your superpowers over zombies!" Amber insisted. "Kyle's right. Keep threatening to cast a spell or use your superpowers."

"If only it were so simple," Zack said. "I'd be stirring my magic cauldron right now."

"Well," Amber said, "if things get hairy tonight, tell him you're going to whip up your powers."

"I think I missed that lesson at Hogwarts," Zack said.

"Okay, Dad!" Amber called. "Look, Dad wants to go for ice cream, so I gotta run. But you guys be careful, okay?"

"Going out for ice cream at ten o'clock?" Zack asked. "Your dad is way cool."

"He's okay." Amber lowered her voice. "Just call me as soon as you get up in the morning!"

After we hung up, I stretched out on my bed and opened up my Freaky Files. Somehow, I hoped I would find a new hook, a new piece of info that would give us an easy way to stop Lassiter. Cards and photos fell out. I sorted through stuff about alien invaders from Roswell and mummies who came alive in Egyptian tombs. I knew this stuff by heart. The answer wasn't here.

I changed into my sweats and a T-shirt, then went downstairs and said good night to everyone. Up in my room, I stuffed a line of pillows under my comforter. The human dummy. In case anyone looked in, they'd think I was asleep.

*Not bad,* I thought as I stepped back.

I crept down the stairs, trying to avoid the creaky spots. The television was on in the den. Pausing on the landing, I listened to the conversation. Gramma and Mom were talking about where to hang the new mirror.

"I like it above the fireplace," Mom said, "but that spot's a bit high for a mirror. I was thinking of the hallway."

"That's an idea," Gramma agreed. "I think the frame would be a nice contrast to the wallpaper there."

Big yawn. I was glad they hadn't asked me to watch TV with them.

Outside, I grabbed my scooter from under the porch and wheeled it quietly down the walk. I hopped on at the corner and started cruising.

That was when my cell phone bleeped. I snapped it open, expecting Zack to abort our mission.

"Hey, Kyle! I just had this great idea," Tommy said.

I paused. "Do you know what time it is?" Then I felt a stab of panic. "Wait! You didn't call my house looking for me, did you?"

"No way! I never call the 'rents' phone after nine. It's one of my rules."

"Good thing," I said, imagining Mom flinging my pillow dummy aside. "Look, Tommy, I really can't talk."

"You'll want to hear this. What if we cover the zombies with paint? You know how they do that in the movies? They pour a big bucket of paint over the ghost, and suddenly you can see its form. Like Nick's green slime. That way, we can go on TV and —"

"It's not going to work, Tommy."

"How do you know if you haven't tried it?"

"Just trust me on this. These are zombies, not ghosts. And it's not like the movies." That was one lesson I was learning, big-time. Tommy was quiet. "You there?"

"Well, look at that," he said. "Marshmallow Margolis is sneaking out."

"What! What?" Already I knew what was happening. Tommy lived across the street from Zack. He was probably looking out the window now.

"That's right, good old Zack is taking off on his bike," Tommy said slyly. "I'll give you one more chance to come clean. He *is* the Zack who saw the zombies, right? Right?"

"No! No, it wasn't him," I said, though I could hear the false note in my voice.

"I don't know, Kyle," Tommy said. "You're holding out on me. I can feel it."

I stepped back onto my scooter and coasted. Zack was going to be waiting for me. "Look, Tommy, I have to go. Call me tomorrow and I'll tell you more about the zombies."

"Trying to get rid of me, Kyle?"

"No, really! We'll talk in the morning."

"Whatever." He hung up.

I tucked my phone in my pocket and scooted away furiously. I could see Zack ahead. He was waiting in the neon light of Pizza Pizzazz. He was wearing his jacket and a backpack, and he didn't look too happy.

"You know, we could ditch the cemetery and grab a slice inside," he said, nodding toward the pizza place.

I shook my head. "We have to do this. What's in here?" I asked, patting the backpack.

"I brought us flashlights and some snacks and juice boxes."

"Flashlights?" I squinted. "So we can, what? Signal the zombies?"

"Oh, like I'm supposed to know what to bring on a zombie stakeout?"

I had to bite my lips to hide a smile. "I don't

think I've had a juice box since kindergarten. I mean, water, yeah. Or soda, mm-hmm." I couldn't help it, I had to grin. "Did you bring us little animal crackers? I used to love those things."

"You know," Zack rolled his eyes, "if you fell in a grave and got stuck there for a week, you'd be pretty darned happy to have some Juicy Juice on hand."

"No, man, it's cool," I said, holding up one hand. "Juice is good. Set your autopilot on the old graveyard and let's roll."

We went for a block or so, then I turned toward Zack. "And just so you know, Tommy saw you sneak out."

"Just now?" Zack winced. "That guy won't leave me alone."

"He wants to be your friend," I said. "Sort of."

"Great. Now he's got something to hold over my head."

"I'll talk to him," I said. "But I wish I had some-thing, like that neuralyzer in *Men in Black II*. Remember that? One flash and your memory goes blank. It'd be so cool to do that to Tommy."

"To Tommy?" Zack muttered. "I want you to do it to *me*. I'd love to forget these zombies ever came." He rolled up to the graveyard gate and hit the brakes.

I stepped off my scooter beside him. "When do you think they'll take this old fence down?" The graveyard was surrounded by a wrought-iron fence. A tall one, with spikes at the top. It added to the creepy look of the place.

Zack shrugged. "I don't know. But I still can't imagine going to school where the old graveyard used to be. I mean, even though they moved the bodies —"

"Some of the bodies didn't want to be moved," I finished for him. "We know that." I took my scooter over by a gnarled tree. "Let's leave our wheels here."

Zack walked his bike over. "Let me go on record as saying this is a very bad idea."

"I'll make a note in my Freaky Files," I said. "When I get home."

"*If* you get home."

"Relax!" I said. "This is a small mission. And you know that the zombies are afraid of us. Or at least Lassiter is. Remember what Amber said? He's afraid we'll turn our magic on him."

Zack was silent for a minute. "I don't know.

Lassiter still went after your grandmother in the yard . . ."

Sometimes Zack is way too logical. "Superpowers. We got 'em, and we're standing by 'em."

"Okay, Spiderman," Zack said. "Just so you know, I don't fly, and I'm just like Cinderella. I've got to be home by midnight or I totally lose my powers."

"Very funny."

A crescent moon was high in the sky. It lit the weird landscape. With the coffins and grave markers gone, the place looked like a rolling wave of hills. There were still mounds of dirt. Sections of chalky red clay. Clumps of grass.

I stepped up onto a mound of dirt but my foot sank in. Down . . . down.

"Whoa!" I yelped, jumping back.

"Watch your step, Super Kyle. You don't want to fall," Zack warned me. "Falling into graveyard dirt is not a memory at the top of my wish list."

Walking past a tree that had been spared, I shivered. "This is like walking on another planet."

"Shh!" Zack crept along beside me. "We're going to find a hiding place, right?"

"Right," I said, looking up at a tree with some low, thick branches. "How about this? If we climb up past the first bough, no one will be able to see us in those leaves."

Zack gave it a thought, then nodded. I boosted him up past the part with no handholds. Then he reached down to help me up. We settled side by side on the fork of a branch.

"This is crazy," he whispered.

"And it's about to get crazier," I said, feeling a flicker of excitement. We were on a mission.

Leaves shimmered in the breeze. The area around us had been flattened out. The hill at the back of the cemetery remained, but now part of it dropped off sharply. It looked like one of the bulldozers had carved out a hunk of hill. A mini-cliff, maybe eight feet high.

"Look, over there," Zack whispered, pointing to the sloping hill.

Something moved at the crest. Something human.

No, it was something dead.

A cloaked head rose above the horizon. As we watched, the figure grew taller. A hooded cape was draped around the bones. Bones so sharp, you'd swear he was a walking skeleton. He seemed to emerge from the ground, his arms rising to the moon.

As if he were sucking up the moonlight.

Then he swept his arms over the land. He pointed down to the ravine. A line of light seemed to connect him to the land. The light beam grew stronger, but it was an eerie red.

"Do you see that?" Zack whispered.

"Yeah," I whispered back. "And I sure hope he doesn't see us."

# CHAPTER SEVEN

**O**h, man," Zack gave a moan. "That thing is the creepiest. He's like a vampire zombie. Or a warlock."

"Did he just throw a lightning bolt?" I asked, my palms itching against the bark.

"I don't know. First of all, it was red, and the guy can't shoot lightning from his hands, can he?"

I closed my eyes and thought about it.

Freaky Files Entry: Superheroes who shoot from the hand.

Spiderman — shoots a web from his wrist.

Lightning Joe — picks lightning bolts out of the sky and tosses them like spears.

Captain Bond — squirts glue from his magic ring.

"Kyle?" Zack said. "If that was real lightning, isn't this tree the worst place to be?"

I looked up at the sky, but it was hard to see around the red leaves. "It wasn't supposed to rain," I said.

"Kyle? Are you scared?"

My heart was hammering in my chest. Other than that, I was cool. "Of course not," I insisted. "I'm just thinking. I was —"

"Shh. He's coming."

I pressed my cheek against the rough tree bark as the cloaked one moved closer. Unlike the other zombies, who plodded along, this guy seemed to float. He went over to a mound of dirt and probed it with a stick.

"What's he doing?" I whispered.

Zack didn't answer. I think he was too scared.

Trying to ignore my racing heart, I watched.

The cloaked zombie pressed his staff deep into the pile of mushy dirt. Suddenly, the mound cracked like an egg. Dirt exploded in the air as Lassiter jumped up, shaking himself like a wet dog.

Now the cloaked zombie came close to our tree. Closer . . . closer . . .

Had he spotted us? Was he coming to get us?

I held my breath as he floated by. He tapped a pile of dirt near the entrance — the same mound of mud I'd nearly sunk into. The dirt scattered, and the zombie in the lab coat sprang to life.

"Oh, man," I breathed. "I almost stepped on him."

Zack winced and swallowed hard. He looked like he'd hit what I call "phase two fear." That's the dazed phase, when the fear squeezes you tight and you dig in and prepare for the worst.

I was getting there myself. My heart was racing like a train, but I tried to take deep, even breaths. I couldn't let fear swallow me up. If I raced out of here like a blubbering kid, Lassiter would win. He'd be right back in my yard tomorrow, scratching Gramma . . . and who knew who else. He'd be roaming around town putting the whammy on kids. He'd be trying to capture a human slave.

I had to hold it together.

The graveyard came alive around us. Zombies staggered toward the center of the clearing. Dirt clumps crumbled from their ragged bodies.

The zombie with the stick was tapping a third mud hill, but nothing was happening.

"Awaken, child," he said. His voice was a dry, chalky whisper.

At last, the dirt exploded and Sky popped up, stretching. I guess she liked to sleep in. Typical zombie kid.

Each zombie hoisted a boulder or log and carried it over to the clearing. The zombies definitely had it in the strength department. They gathered around a shiny patch of black. Squinting, I realized it was a puddle.

When they were all seated, the cloaked zombie stood up and lifted his stick to the sky. Another bolt of red light traveled down to the stick. He was all aglow as he pointed the stick at the puddle. And — *zap* — a crescent moon glowed there, like a reflection.

Now the puddle was so bright, it lit the zombies' chalky faces. I couldn't take my eyes off it.

"I do not like being pulled from sleep," Sky complained. She tossed her long hair back. The moonlight seemed to fall into her hole of a nose. "Do not do it again."

"You will do as you are told, girl," Lassiter told her.

"I never wanted to come here!" she insisted. "I was looking for the colony."

"Enough," the cloaked zombie said. His voice was a raspy whisper. I strained to hear. "We are assembled to go forward with the plan. I understand Mr. Lassiter has found a candidate?"

Lassiter nodded. The ax bobbed. "Yes, yes,

this one is perfect. She was in charge of a school. Smart and practical, with a strong mind. A solid build, too. She'll do just fine."

I felt my throat tighten. "He's talking about my grandmother," I whispered.

Zack winced but waved his hand at me to be quiet.

"I must see her," the cloaked zombie said. "Then we can proceed." I still hadn't seen his face, but his voice had a slight accent. Like a British gentleman.

"There is one problem, Mr. Dread," Lassiter said, rubbing his bony hands together, "Right now there's a boy near her. And he has a spell . . . the power to send us back."

"What is this power?" asked the one called Dread.

Lassiter grunted. "I don't know. I don't understand it. But they have a spell to make us disappear."

"Really?" Dread seemed amused. "I have used such a spell myself." He pointed his staff at Sky. "How do you think that colony disappeared, after all?"

"Roanoke didn't disappear," Sky insisted. "I

simply couldn't find it. I lost my way while crossing the river."

I didn't know what she was talking about, but she sounded so lost. For a second I felt sorry for her. Until I remembered that she was a zombie, and she was part of the group planning to enslave my gramma. *Remember, Kyle? That pitiful zombie girl wants to eat your gramma's brains.*

Lassiter stood up and tossed a dirt clod into the puddle. Sparks of light skittered over the surface. "I'm just saying, the boy and his friends are trouble."

"If I may say, Mr. Lassiter," the guy in the lab coat jumped in. "I was acclaimed as one of the finest minds of my time. Perhaps you underestimate my intelligence?"

Lassiter waved a hand at him. "But you're already dead, boyo!"

"Indeed. There is power in the legend," Dread said in his hushed tone. *"A single human shall lead the dead."*

Lassiter growled and tossed his head back. *"We will hunt, we will scour, till the day we find the one living human to lead zombiekind!"*

"Kyle!" Zack squeezed my arm. His eyes were

white and googly-wide in the darkness. "The poem! That's the one Penelope recited."

"It must be an old legend," I said. "They probably think it's their destiny." And from my experience gathering the Freaky Files, I knew there had to be more to it. Some brew to concoct. Some spell or superpower. Usually there was a whole list of things they would need to make their plan work.

"We must proceed with swift and sure measure," Dread rasped. "If the gentlewoman is the chosen, we must take care to keep her alive. She may slip into a deep sleep, but never may the spirit leave the body. Otherwise, she is useless to us."

"Okay." I gulped. "At least they're not going to kill her."

"Right," Zack said, shifting the straps of the backpack. "They're just going to put her in a trance so they can eat her brain or something."

I couldn't believe I was watching this. A bunch of dead guys were planning to turn my grandmother into a zombie! "Would you pinch me?" I said to Zack. "Because this is one supremo nightmare, and I'd like to wake up."

"And it's about to get worse," Zack said, pointing. I followed his finger to the short cliffs, just beyond the zombies. "Tommy Hernandez. What's *he* doing here?"

Sure enough, Tommy stood casually on one of the small bluffs. He had his hands in his sweatshirt pockets, and he was gawking at the zombies.

Okay, I admit, a group of undead gathered around a shining puddle is quite a sight. But didn't Tommy realize that *they* would be able to see *him,* too?

"He's nuts!" I whispered. But it was worse than I thought. Tommy kept moving closer to the edge, like a little kid edging closer to the water.

Then it happened. Tommy must have walked over a weak spot, because suddenly the ground gave way. He grabbed at the air, but it was no use. Down he went, tumbling in a shower of mud and rocks.

"Oh, great!" Zack gasped. "Now he's definitely dead meat!"

The sudden noise stopped Lassiter in his tracks. All the zombies turned toward Tommy, who had landed on all fours.

I smacked my forehead. "Aw, man! They see him. He'll never get away now!"

The zombies rose and began marching toward Tommy.

"A young spy?" Dread asked.

"I've seen this one before," Lassiter said.

Tommy held his hands up as the zombies surrounded him. "Dead dudes! I come in peace!" he squeaked. His face was pale as he pressed against the side of the cliff.

"He's a troublemaker," Lassiter said. "Let's get him!"

"Nooo!" Tommy wailed as the zombies edged closer.

# CHAPTER EIGHT

"All right, then," I said, trying to sound more casual than I felt. "Any ideas on how to get Tommy out of this jam?"

Zack slid off his backpack and started unzipping. "I knew this stuff would come in handy," he said.

"Zack, man, this is no time for juice!"

"The flashlights," he said. "Remember how the zombies freaked when we flicked the light switch the first time? Lassiter may be catching on, but the others might still be scared." He took out the flashlights.

I blinked. "It might work. Although Dread seems to have his own light-saber thing going on. What else do you have in there?" I started routing through his backpack. Past the extra sweater. The juice boxes. The cans of Cheez Whiz . . .

"Whoa, wait!" I said. "You brought Cheez Whiz?"

"I thought we might get hungry."

"It's perfect! We can shoot it at the zombies while we shine the light in their faces!"

Zack frowned. "Do you really think zombies are afraid of cheese?"

"No, but they probably won't know what it is!" I stuck one can in my pocket, then handed him the other. "Let's roll!"

I slid down from the tree. Zack was right behind me. Slowly, we edged toward the zombies. We turned on the flashlights and pressed them against our jackets to hide the light. Then, trigger fingers on the Whiz, we moved toward the group.

"Let's extract his brain," Dr. Zombie said. "He would make a marvelous specimen for a study."

"Oh, I hate to do it!" Sky complained. "He was so kind to me. This is the boy who shared his corn."

"That's right!" Tommy gasped. "I'm a nice guy. Right, Sky? Tell them!"

"You were very sweet," she agreed. "But I cannot help you, boy. As my father used to say, it's a good day to die. A brave warrior welcomes death."

"No!" Tommy held up his hands, as if that would stop the march of the zombies.

"Oh, come now," Mr. Dread said in a calming voice.

Tommy lowered his hands.

Dread reached a finger forward, and I noticed his nail was long and sharp. Like a dagger. He poked at Tommy's cheek. "There's plenty of meat on this one's bones," he rasped quietly. "Plenty for all of us."

"Hey!" Tommy slapped his hand away. Dread growled.

"Now!" I told Zack.

"Aaargh!" I yelled, plunging forward.

"Eeeeerrr!" Zack shrieked. He was right behind me.

We swung the flashlights wildly. The beams of light danced through the air.

Now for the Big Cheesing.

I ran up to Dr. Zombie and pressed the nozzle. A string of cheese shot into his rotting face. I squirted and squirted.

"Aaargh!" He shook his head back and forth, waving his arms.

"What is happening?" Sky gasped. "An attack? I cannot —" Her words were garbled when Zack squirted a glob of cheese into her rotten mouth.

Zack was still working on Sky as I swung toward Lassiter. Tommy was right next to him. He looked too stunned to move.

"What's this?" Lassiter's lone eye glimmered with suspicion.

"It's part of our spell," I said forcefully. I held up the can of Cheese Whiz. "Part of our power comes from this can!"

Lassiter backed away. "Do not use it on me!" He pressed into the clay wall.

"Sorry, dude." I pointed it at him. "Like she said, it's a good day to die!"

"No!" He backed into the cliff.

I have to admit, it felt great to cheese Lassiter. He turned and began to dig with his gnarled fingernails. That guy scratched away like crazy. And since zombies are pretty strong, he'd made a decent-size hole in the dirt wall when I felt something sharp in my back.

"Eeow!" I whirled around.

It was the prick of Dread's fingernail, right through my jacket.

Zack was cheesing him from behind, but Dread didn't seem to care. I shined my light into his face. The flat, chalky skull-face was expressionless. The only sign of life was in his eyes. Red, glowing eyes. They creeped me out.

"Okay," I stammered. "Time to go."

"Come on, Tommy," Zack yelled, motioning him over.

Tommy snapped to his senses and ran over to Zack.

"Sorry to cheese and run," I told Dread. Pointing carefully under his hood, I sprayed. Orange cheese zigzagged across his skull. I shot him a smiley face on top of that for good measure. Probably the first smile on his face in a century or so. Then I turned and ran.

As Gramma always says, never overstay your welcome.

"Okay, Jackson, let me get this straight," Tommy said as he walked alongside us. We were a safe distance away from the cemetery, but the rush of adrenaline was just letting up. "The kid you were talking about was Zack Margolis. So you lied to me."

"Is that all you can say?" I let myself coast ahead a few feet, then paused. "How about, 'Thanks for saving me, Kyle'?"

"Yeah," Zack added, "or, 'Sorry I fell into that pack of zombies and nearly got us all turned into dead meat.'"

"Yeah, all that, sure," Tommy said. He picked at a clump of hardened clay on his sweatshirt. "But why didn't you just tell me the truth before?"

"Tommy," I said, "don't make me wonder if that was a waste of Cheez Whiz."

"Okay, okay." Tommy waved his hands. "Don't go all parental on me. Sheesh. I know where I'm not wanted."

I sighed. I admit, Tommy can be a total pain in the neck sometimes. But maybe that came from being left out all the time.

Was I one of those kids who kept him on the outside? Sometimes I treated him like he was the annoying kid. Wasn't I always trying to stop him from pushing his way in?

I looked at the near-empty can of Cheez Whiz in my hand. Maybe *I* deserved a good cheesing.

"Tommy . . ." Zack wheeled his bike slowly. "It's not you. When the zombies first came, we didn't want anyone to know about them. We still don't."

"Yeah, well, too late for that," Tommy said, lifting his chin.

"Right," I said. "But now that you know, I mean, *really* know, you're one of us, man. Any guy who's survived zombie combat ought to be in the squad." I turned to Zack. "Right?"

Zack shrugged. "Sure."

"Don't do me any favors," Tommy said, stuffing his hands into his sweatshirt. "I'm not a charity case, Jackson."

"That's not how it is," I insisted. "Look, I'll call you in the morning. First thing."

"Yeah, yeah." Tommy's face was bright red. "Take your Cheez Whiz and hit the road," he said, backing away.

Before I could say anything else, Tommy turned and tramped toward his house.

"I feel awful," Zack said. "First zombie warfare. And now Tommy's upset. Did we do that?"

I bit my lower lip, not really sure. "I'll talk to him tomorrow," I said, hoping I could fix things.

"Wait," Zack said. "What are you going to do about your grandmother? How are you going to protect her from Lassiter?"

"I'm not sure," I admitted. "But I figure I'll start by keeping her in the house."

Zack nodded. "Sounds like a plan. Call me if you need backup."

He turned his bike down his block, and I glided off on my scooter. The neighborhood was still and eerie. Streetlights loomed, but houses were dark. Dark, silent boxes.

I was relieved to see that my house was also dark when I rolled up the driveway. I sucked in my breath as I stole up the porch stairs. I couldn't afford to make a sound.

My key whispered in the lock. I pressed the knob to the left so it wouldn't squeak.

Once inside, I stepped out of my shoes and slid along on my socks. I waited for my eyes to adjust to the shadowed darkness.

Good, everyone was asleep. I crept down the hall, to the bottom of the stairs. I was about to go up, but I paused.

I had to check on Gramma. Just a peek to know she was okay.

I leaned against the den door frame. Barely breathing, I dropped my head into the open doorway.

The room was filled by the open sofa bed. My eyes traveled over the old blue suitcase. The smooth blanket. The plumped pillows.

The bed was empty.

Panic shot through me. Gramma was missing!

# CHAPTER NINE

**O**h, man! It couldn't be.

How could the zombies get her so fast, when I just saw them and . . . ?

My heart began to beat hard. It clanged in my chest.

I stepped into the den to make sure. Maybe she'd dozed off in the chair.

No. Gramma was gone — kidnapped by those monsters. I had to wake up my parents and give them the horrible news.

I spun around as something creaked behind me. Gramma stood there, arms crossed.

"Ah!" I gasped, startled.

"Aha is right, child," she said. "I don't mind telling you, you nearly gave your old gramma a heart attack."

I was snagged. Totally busted. Gramma had caught me. But I was never so happy to see her small round frame in her red and purple silk robe.

"What are you thinking, sneaking out of the house late at night? Have you got any brains left, boy? Or is that head full of videotapes and computer games?"

I touched my head. Sort of a reflex. "It's not that, Gramma. I just —"

"You just better jump-start the mind God gave you and start using it!"

"I will. I'm sorry."

"Sorry isn't good enough when you're an eleven-year-old boy out on his own near midnight." She put her hands on her hips. "Where were you?"

I didn't know what to tell her. The truth? Like she'd believe that. "I was with my friend Zack," I said. "And . . . and another friend."

She nodded, her eyebrows a stern line under her smooth bangs. "Go on."

"And . . ." I noticed the tiny scrape on her chin. The mark from Lassiter's grubby fingernail. Suddenly, the idea of that creep hurting Gramma made me buckle inside. I couldn't stand it if the zombies hurt her. "Oh, Gramma . . ." I closed my eyes and pressed my face against the shoulder of her robe. "What if something bad happens to you?"

"Your gramma is just fine," she said. I felt her arms surround me, warm and secure. "Besides, we take the bad with the good, child."

She wouldn't say that if she could see Isaac Lassiter.

"Don't think you're going to distract your gramma by changing the subject," she added, rubbing my back. "What have you been up to?"

I tried to pull together an excuse that had a grain of truth. Otherwise, she'd nail me. Gramma had a vision for the truth. "I snuck out to hang with my friends," I said. "Really. And we didn't do anything wrong."

"Mmm-hmm. As if it's not wrong to sneak out at all hours."

"Well, I meant, once we were out. It was just that . . . my friend Tommy needed some help with . . . with his research. It's sort of a group project."

"Either it *is* or it *isn't*," she said. "When are you going to wipe that 'sort of' business out of your vocabulary?"

I was about to answer, "Whatever," but I knew it would only make things worse. "Sorry, ma'am," I said. "I meant, it's something we're working on together."

"Mmm-hmm." She leaned back to look me in the eye. "And what's the topic?"

"It's . . . Isaac Lassiter." I was proud of myself. Hung that one on the truth. "He's this bad dude. Been dead awhile. We're doing a biography on him."

"And you'll have me believe the library is open this late on Friday nights?"

"No, Gramma." Think fast, I thought. Then, "We've been trying online, but so far just dead ends."

"Hmm." She stretched her hands out. "Perhaps you're not looking in the right places?" She glanced toward the den. "Should we boot up and give it a shot?"

"Sure," I said, a little surprised. I never thought of my grandmother using a computer, but — whatever.

We huddled in front of the computer in the dark den. The screen made her face glow blue, but she looked happy. Like a kid playing with a toy.

Gramma's secret weapon was a special search engine. She was a subscriber. She had a password to gain access. From there, she cruised down the information superhighway.

It took a while. I admit, I smothered a few yawns. But Gramma was relentless. She didn't give up until she got a hit.

"There! Your Mr. Lassiter is mentioned in a poem. It's called 'All for a Bundle of Gold.'"

I squinted at the screen. "Cool! Where's the poem?"

"Unfortunately we can't access it online. But if you go to the library tomorrow, I'm sure you'll find it in this book called *Ballads of Infamous Men*."

I shook my head. "We already checked the library. We didn't get any hits when we plugged his name into the reference computer."

"Sometimes, when books are catalogued, it's not possible to lift every name mentioned in that book. Your Mr. Lassiter is a prime example. He wasn't even in the poem's title, certainly not in the title of the book. But the poem is subtitled 'The Ballad of Isaac Lassiter.'"

"That's definitely him," I said. "I hope the book is there."

"I'm sure it's in the collection," Gramma said. "Bess Grimble always took pride in stocking books about local history. There's a special section for it."

I nodded. I'd been there, done that, but I hadn't noticed this book. "I'll look for it tomorrow. Thanks, Gramma."

"It's late," Gramma said. "Off to bed with you."

I stuck the Post-it note with the book information to my sleeve and stretched.

Gramma squinted at me, then touched my jacket. "What's this orange stuff?" She rubbed her fingers together, then held them to her nose. "Oh, child, it smells nasty."

I didn't think she'd appreciate how effective a weapon Cheez Whiz could be. So I just said, "I'll throw it in the wash. Good night, Gramma." I headed upstairs.

I totally zonked out that night. Who knew that zombie fighting took so much energy? In the morning, I felt fortified by Dad's traditional Saturday pancakes and the hit Gramma had gotten on the computer. I called Amber and Zack with the news.

"What a great lead, O Wizard of Cheese," Amber said over the phone.

"Hey, I brought the Cheez Whiz," Zack said. "Don't I get any credit?"

"Absolutely," Amber said. "I always knew your snack attacks would pay off one day."

As I talked, I slid a black tie around my collar. "Let's meet at the Curl & Twirl. Gramma wants to get her hair done for the ceremony, so I can go into town with her. I want to stick by her while she's there."

"We'll help you Gramma-sit," Amber said. "Remember, Lassiter still thinks we have superpowers. If we're all there, he'll be too afraid to come near her."

"I hope we can find that book at the library," Zack said. "I can't wait to send him off to the next level."

Freaky Files Entry: The Next Level — it's the place dead people go — sort of like eternal rest, I guess. Most people seem to make the voyage there without a problem when they die. But the zombies are people who got stuck here. We sent Jeremiah to the next level, then Chastity. And when it happens, it is *so* cool. They look really happy. And they transform. For a second, before they POOF off into glittery dust, they turn back into their younger, healthier selves. Their skin is bright and smooth, their teeth and hair shiny.

"Yeah," I told my friends, "Lassiter doesn't

realize we'd be doing him a favor. I am so ready to send him off — with a one-way ticket."

After we hung up, I finished getting dressed, then hit the Freaky Files. I was so sure that there was something to learn there — that the key to Lassiter could be found in the papers and cards and articles I'd collected.

In all my Files, there was nothing about a guy with an ax in his back.

Not a lot of lumberjack horror films.

But as I flipped through Horror Film Fan Cards, I hit something.

It was a movie called *The Wheat Walks*. The creatures weren't really zombies. They were walking, talking scarecrows.

As I sank back on my bed, the story came back to me. These scarecrows were actually men who had died in prison. They turned into scarecrows because they had never been tried for their crimes. The Emperor of the Wheat gave each scarecrow a trial. If the scarecrow was guilty, he stayed a scarecrow. If the scarecrow was innocent, he was turned back into a man.

I pulled out an index card to make a note. I put all my notes on the computer now, but since Gramma was in the den, that would have to wait.

Freaky Files Entry: Scarecrow prisoners from *The Wheat Walks* — prisoners turn into scarecrows so they can get a trial.

I bit my lower lip. Lassiter never had a trial. Maybe that was his problem. Justice had not been carried out.

Hmm. If it was a trial he needed, the Zombie Squad could help him out.

I was sifting through my notes about a movie called *Attack of the Killer Tomatoes* when Gramma called my name.

"Kyle! I'm ready to go."

I went to the top of the stairs.

"Do you still want a ride into town?" she asked.

I bounded down the stairs. "Gramma, it's only a few blocks. We can walk."

"Not today. I want to visit with friends, and I have errands. There'll be too much to carry back. Now, say good-bye to your parents before you make me late. It's not easy to get a Saturday appointment at the Curl & Twirl."

"Okay," I said, smiling. I'd never been cruising in Gramma's red Cadillac. I said good-bye to my parents and followed Gramma out the side door.

"Do you have the information on that book you wanted?" Gramma asked, going down the porch stairs to the driveway.

I sensed that something was wrong. Then I saw them.

Lassiter and Dread.

They waited for her at the bottom of the steps, their rotting faces gruesome in the warm morning sun. They had come for Gramma.

# CHAPTER TEN

I wanted to pull Gramma back into the house, but I knew I couldn't keep her inside forever. Instead, I hurried after her, wondering how to protect her. Would they try to capture her now? Were they going to try to put her to sleep or cast a spell?

"At last, our lady approaches," Dread whispered. He bowed as Gramma stepped near him. "She looks like a fine candidate, indeed."

"Kyle!" Gramma called. "Did you hear me? Do you have the title of that book you need?"

"Yes, Gramma," I said. "I have it." I wanted to say to Lassiter: "Information on the book that will help us send you out of here. Spiraling through space to another dimension." How I would love to shut him down! But I didn't want to tip my hand.

As Gramma got into the car, I went around to the other side, muttering to Lassiter and Dread.

"Why don't you guys get lost?" I said. "Just back off!"

Lassiter smiled, and, though I couldn't see Dread's face, he wasn't exactly quivering with fear. "You'll be much better off if you just stand back and let us take what we need," Lassiter said. He pulled the ax out of his back and tested the blade with one crusty fingernail. "Nice and sharp."

"You're bluffing," I said, remembering what they'd said in the zombie circle. They needed her alive. But that wasn't much consolation with two dead ghouls lurking in my driveway. I didn't wait around for zombie chitchat. I just jumped into Gramma's car and closed the door behind me. It felt good to leave them standing in the driveway. Maybe now my knees would stop shaking.

Outside the salon, Gramma whipped the car into a spot and slid her handbag onto her arm. "Come along," she said, "Nellie will want to see you."

"Well, look at you!" an older woman cried as we stepped inside. Nellie tucked her scissors and comb into one hand and rushed over. "You've stayed away too long, girl! How's South Carolina?"

"Just fine," Gramma said as she hugged the woman. Although they were around the same age, Nellie was a stick compared to Gramma. "Nellie, this is my grandson, Kyle."

Nellie turned her big brown eyes on me. "I don't believe it! Last time I saw him, you were chasing him around the yard. Dinah, you can't have a grandson this tall."

I cringed, expecting Nellie to pinch my cheeks.

"Mmm-hmm," Gramma murmured. "He's Marcus's son. Say hello to Mrs. Wilson, Kyle."

"It's nice to meet you," I said, holding out my hand.

"What a fine, young boy," Nellie said, shaking my hand. "Let me finish up Mary's cut here. Sarah will get you washed."

While Gramma slipped off her sweater, I sat down in a plastic chair. The smell in the Curl & Twirl is pretty awful. Hair dyes and straighteners. I don't know how Nellie can stand those chemicals. Then again, I guess you get used to it. Like being around the zombies.

"Don't you have somewhere to go?" Gramma asked me. "What about the library?"

"That's okay," I said, figuring I could stick around and do zombie patrol. "I don't mind waiting here."

"But I mind," Gramma said as Sarah led her over to a sink. "Do you think these ladies want you hanging around while their hair is in curlers?"

Not something I wanted to see. But I had to protect Gramma.

She sat down, staring at me as Sarah wrapped a towel around her neck. "Go on, Kyle. This is no place for a boy your age."

That was for sure. If the smell didn't get you, the weirdo photos of haircuts would. Dreads and cornrows were one thing. But there was actually a man who'd had the Philly Fliers emblem shaved into his 'fro.

I glanced over at Nellie. Did Gramma's friend know how to carve sports logos into guys' heads?

"Kyle!" Gramma turned to Nellie. "Sometimes you'd think the boy was deaf."

"Mmm-hmm. They're all that way," Nellie said. "It's their age."

"Okay, Gramma," I said, backing toward the door. "I'll be outside when you're done."

When I got outside, Amber and Zack were coming up the street.

"Hey, man," Zack said, scratching his cheek. He was wearing a visor that said FLORIDA STATE. That's where he used to live. He moved here just before the school year started. Zack wasn't thrilled to give up surfing and water-skiing for boring old Paxituckett. But since the zombies followed him home, I hadn't heard Zack complain about being bored. Not even once.

"Let's hit the library," Zack said.

I peered into the salon through the big glass window. "I'm not sure. Lassiter and the new one, Dread, were outside the house when we left. Dread agreed that Gramma is a fine candidate for a human slave."

"I can't wait to eyeball that creep." Amber pushed back her baseball cap and took a rubber ball from her pocket. "I say we split up. Zack, why don't you do the library? Kyle and I will stay here on granny watch."

Zack was cool with that. I gave him the book info, and he headed off.

Amber followed the line of the building to

the side alley. "Let's wait over here," she said, bouncing the rubber ball against the wall.

"So you can practice your handball?" I asked.

"Exactly." She twirled and backhanded the ball. "Do you think your gramma knows something is up?"

I turned over an empty crate and sat on it. "She caught me sneaking in last night."

"Ouch."

"Yeah, and with Cheez Whiz on my jacket. I didn't even *try* to explain that one."

"I've been thinking about Lassiter," Amber said. "About what his key issue might be. I'm sure it has something to do with the guy he killed."

"I was thinking the same thing," I said.

"What if it's revenge?" Amber suggested. "What if Lassiter can't rest until he gets revenge on the guy who killed him?"

I frowned. "That could be messy." Lassiter's killer was definitely dead. How could a dead man get revenge on another dead man? This was getting way too dead, even for me.

"I was going through the Freaky Files," I said, "and I hit on this movie about scarecrows. The scarecrows died while they were awaiting trial.

The whole point was that justice had to be done. What if that's the hang-up with Lassiter?"

Amber cupped the ball under her chin. "And he needs a trial?" She winced. "That would be awful. We could never pull together a zombie trial."

"Why not?" I asked. "Okay, the same players wouldn't be there. But we could read the charges from the sheriff's logbook. And we could read witness statements, if we could find them."

She smiled. "Wow, your dad's work is really growing on you."

"No, all the legal stuff is from the TV shows we watch. But what do you think?"

Her freckled face puckered up as she thought about it. "I like it. Hey, anything that might get rid of Lassiter is worth a try."

She turned and started bouncing the ball again.

"I just don't know how we would get Lassiter to his own trial," I said. "He's so different from the others. Jeremiah and Chastity *wanted* to have their problems fixed . . . ."

"Hey, Jackson!" Tommy called. He was ambling up the street. "Thanks for the phone call, man."

I turned around, trying not to wince. "Tommy." I'd completely forgotten. "Hey, whassup?"

"A couple of dead people," Tommy said, his eyes shining in his chipmunk face. "They're going to be up in New York for the morning shows. Then they'll be flying out to Hollywood to meet Jay Leno."

"Tommy, don't be ticked off," I said.

Amber caught her ball and jumped in. "It's not Kyle's fault. It was all of us. We need to keep it a secret. But now that you know . . ." she shrugged. "That's cool, Tommy. In fact, I was hoping we could count on you for a little help."

Tommy didn't blink. "I'm going public with the zombies," he said. "I'll start at the police station. Then I'll bring them to school to scare Mr. Cavalucci out of his shorts. One way to get out of gym. After that — TV. This is a big story. Huge. Humongous."

"Adults don't see them," I reminded him. "You can't do this, Tommy. It'll only start trouble."

"Too late," Tommy said. "I've already videotaped a few spots with Sky." He shrugged. "She's not so bad with a little makeup."

I felt the breath catch in my throat. Zombies on television. It wouldn't work. It would backfire into a huge mess. Didn't Tommy see that?

"Tommy! Have you totally lost it?" Amber shoved at his shoulder. "Don't be a big pea brain!"

Tommy just stepped away from her. "I'll be rich, I tell you." He let out a laugh like a lunatic. "Rich, rich, rich!"

# CHAPTER ELEVEN

Tommy . . . you can't do this!" I shouted.

With a smug look, Tommy folded his arms. He looked at me. Then at Amber. Then he pointed at us and bellowed, "Gotcha!"

Amber pushed up the sleeves of her jacket. "What?"

"You got us?" I said. "As in, it was all a big prank?"

"A joke!" he insisted. "Ha! And you guys really went for it. Hee-hee!" He laughed. We didn't.

"Right." Amber said, rolling her eyes. "Easy, Tommy. If I laugh any harder, I'll wet my pants. Not!" She turned back to the wall and tossed the ball.

"Let me get this straight. You didn't tell anyone about the zombies?" I asked.

"Who would I tell?" he asked. "The stupid things can't even be seen by grown-ups. You can't get anywhere in the world if you can't get recognized by grown-ups."

"Finally, you're making sense," Amber said.

"Yeah, well . . ." Tommy sat down beside me on the crate. "I don't like it when people lie to me, Kyle." He was watching Amber, but I knew this was all about me.

"I'm sorry," I said. "If it makes you feel any better, you're not the only one. I've had to tell some whoppers to my parents since the zombies came."

"Every kid bends the truth for his parents," Tommy said. "I thought we were friends." He turned toward me. The puppy dog look in his eyes killed me.

"We are friends," I said. "And if you want, you can be totally in on the zombie stuff. We just need to keep things cool."

He turned away. "I can do that."

I was doubtful. But I figured it was time to give Tommy a chance. For a while, we sat and watched Amber slam the ball against the wall.

"How did you know we'd be here?" I asked Tommy.

He shrugged. "Your mom said you went into town. You already saw the movie playing here. You're not mall rats, so I knew you'd be somewhere around the town square." He glanced down the alley. "But what are you guys doing here?"

"We're guarding Kyle's gramma," Amber said.

"The zombies are trying to kidnap her," I explained.

"No way! I don't believe it. Sky wouldn't hurt a sweet old lady."

"Sweet?" Amber said, raising an eyebrow. "Apparently, you haven't met Kyle's gramma."

"Sky may not be totally in on the plot," I said, "but Lassiter and Dread were waiting in my driveway this morning. They need to capture a live human. Someone to lead them."

"Lead them *where?*" Tommy asked.

Even though the guy was too literal, he had a good question. I shrugged. "Lead them to . . . I don't know. Take over the world?"

Tommy looked down the street. "I'd think that was cool — if they hadn't attacked me last night." He worked the zipper of his jacket up and down. "I barely got past them on my way here. I don't think they recognized me. I was moving pretty fast."

"What?" I turned to him. "Who?"

"The two ghouls. The one-eyed ax man and

the grim reaper." He pulled his jacket closer around him. "I passed them a few blocks away, just on the other side of the town square."

"Oh, great," I said. "They're getting close."

"Actually, they were just sitting there," Tommy said. "Like vultures."

"No big," Amber said. "If they find us, we just need to pretend we're going to put a spell on them. That will scare them off for a while."

"A spell?" Tommy frowned. "Like that's going to work."

"Believe me, it will," I said. "You've got some catching up to do, Tommy. Maybe you should come over one day and go over my Freaky Files. I've been documenting everything."

"He even has videotapes of the zombies," Amber said. "Kyle is the Freaky Master."

Just then I heard the sound of sneakers slapping pavement. I stepped out of the alley, and Zack nearly barreled into me.

"Got the book," he said breathlessly. "But I ran into Lassiter and Dread in the square. I ran, but I think they're following me." He sucked in a breath. "They're on their way here."

"Don't worry," Tommy told him. "Amber is going to whip up a spell in her magic cauldron."

Zack shot me a glare. I gave him a look that said: *Give Tommy a break.* "What does the book say?" I asked him.

"I only had time to skim the poem, but it's about Lassiter." Zack opened it to the bookmark. "Ax in the back, lumberjack — it's definitely him."

Just then the salon door jingled open. Gramma stepped out, her hair a smooth cap of ginger red.

"Hello, Mrs. Jackson," Amber said. She'd met Gramma before.

Gramma's eyes went wide. "You've got quite a crowd now, Kyle."

"These are my friends," I said, introducing her to Zack.

"Very nice to meet you all," she said. "It's an odd place for children to play. But I see you've been doing some research." She nodded at the book in Zack's arms.

"Right . . ." Zack flashed me a panicked look. I realized he didn't know the cover story I'd told Gramma.

"For our school project," I said quickly. "The library had the book, and we were just about to read the poem."

**117**

"Then let's hear it," Gramma said, tucking her purse onto her arm. "I have to go over to Mel's to pick up some meat for dinner, then to the florist. But please, read as we go."

"It's called 'All for a Bundle of Gold — the Ballad of Isaac Lassiter,'" Zack said. As we walked across the square, he began to read:

"On the Appalachian Trail came a man
Mean as mean could be,
A lumberjack who made his stand
Despite another's plea.
If truth be told, this man was bold,
He conjured evil undeterred.
He stole another's sack of gold
So goes the Ballad of Lassiter."

As we walked, I listened carefully. Tommy held Zack's shoulders, guiding him so that he could walk and read the long poem. It started with Lassiter coming to Pennsylvania as a young man. A lumberjack.

The work in the forest was hard. Isaac Lassiter wanted a shortcut to riches. One day, a gold miner came through, traveling west. The miner,

Nathan Fuller, was visiting his brother, who worked in the same lumber camp as Lassiter. Isaac Lassiter's eyes lit up when he saw Nathan Fuller's fortune — a sack of gold.

That's when Lassiter turned bad.

According to the legend, Lassiter killed Nathan Fuller for his gold, right in front of two other woodcutters. He was arrested. But before he could stand trial, Lassiter escaped from jail.

(That part we knew, from the sheriff's records.)

"In the local jail was a man
Mean as mean could be
A lumberjack who killed, and then
From prison he did flee.
A woodsman's ax found in his back,
A fitting end for a lumberjack.
His own evil chased him from this world
So goes the Ballad of Lassiter."

We had reached the butcher shop, but no one went inside. We were hooked on Lassiter's story. Not that the poem was so great. But it was creepy to read about a murder, even if it did happen years ago. Zack went on:

"Some say Isaac did himself in,
Crazy with guilt o'er his mortal sin.
Others say it was Jeb Fuller's ax —
The world will never know the facts.
Though the courts may fail,
The ax prevails
To punish evil undeterred.
So goes the Ballad of Lassiter."

"Whoa!" Amber clapped Zack on the back as he finished reading. "That's some story."

"Indeed," Gramma said. "The subject of your biography was a rather gruesome character."

"Gruesome?" came a voice from beyond Mel's Butcher Shop. Lassiter stepped out, his eyeball darting inquisitively. "Did my rotting ears deceive me? There was a ballad written for me?" He pressed his bony hands to his tattered chest. "I'm famous! More notable than Brittany the Spearer!"

"Someone's been hanging out in front of the music store," Amber said, glaring at Lassiter.

"Kyle, I think you children better stay out here." Gramma tugged on the door to Mel's.

I stepped up, barring Lassiter from entering. "Just as long as he stays out here with us," I said.

Gramma shot a frosty look at Zack and nodded. "Yes, I meant all of you. I just need a few things, and Mel doesn't need a gang of children cluttering up the shop." She stepped in, letting the door close behind her.

"Trying to take care of granny?" Lassiter asked me. "I wouldn't bother. Not when I'm your foe. You'll never win against me. Haven't you heard? I'm a local legend. A famous man."

"I think that's *in*famous," Zack corrected.

"I wouldn't be so proud," I told Lassiter. "You're famous because of a murder. Whether or not it's true . . ."

"Oh, it's true." Lassiter licked his mottled lips. "I killed Nathan Fuller for his gold, and I'd do it again, given the chance."

Amber shoved her baseball cap back. "Didn't you learn anything?"

"Indeed, I did," Lassiter hissed. "I learned that you cannot linger near the scene of a crime. I should have taken that gold and gone far, far away." He paced to the store window, where Tommy stood watching.

Tommy put his hands on his hips, a mountain of attitude. "Why don't you just go now?" he asked. "Haul your ratty old bones back to the graveyard."

I was impressed. It was only Tommy's second encounter with a zombie, and he was hanging in there.

Lassiter pushed past him and stared into the butcher shop. "Not without her." He reached back and pulled the ax from his spine. It came loose with a *thwang*!

The blade gleamed in the sunlight.

I felt my throat grow dry. This guy really *was* bad to the bone.

"I've got big plans for her," Lassiter held the ax blade to his chin and grinned. "And I won't be stopped by a bunch of foolish children." He pulled the door open.

But I stepped into his path. "You're not going to hurt her!" I said, glaring into his bloodshot eye. "You need her alive."

He lifted his ax. "Then I'll use the blunt end! A quick blow to knock her out." He clasped his bony fingers around my arm and shoved me aside. I flew into Zack. I'd forgotten about zombies' superstrength.

"Wait!" Amber shouted as Lassiter pushed his way into the butcher shop. Zack helped me back onto my feet, and we hurried in through the doorway.

Lassiter was sitting on the counter in front of Gramma. He held his ax in the air, sizing her up.

Gramma leaned over the zombie's tattered knee. She was eyeing a pork roast on a slab of paper. "That is a fine roast, Mel," she said. "But it's far too much for a family of four. My Marcus doesn't eat the way he used to."

Just then the phone rang. "Excuse me," Mel said, dodging behind the tall glass cases of meat to answer it.

Gramma leaned close to the roast. "Maybe if we cut it in half . . ."

Lassiter raised his ax high. It hovered over Gramma's head.

Oh, man!

"Gramma!" I shouted.

"The spell!" Amber said. "Stop or we'll do the spell!" She was threatening Lassiter, but he didn't seem to hear her.

The zombie swung the ax up . . .

Then down . . .

The ax blade glimmered as it sliced through the air, heading for Gramma's neck!

# CHAPTER TWELVE

**G**ramma!" I shouted again. The ax fell in a deadly arc ... just as Gramma backed away from the counter.

The ax slammed down, chopping the meat in two.

Gramma was already chastising me, hands on her hips. "What are you doing in here?" When she heard the thud, she turned back toward the counter. "What was that?"

Lassiter pulled his ax away and turned toward me. "Next time, stay out of my way, boy!" he growled. "Or I'll take you, too!"

Gramma looked down at the meat. "I wonder if we should go with the larger cut ... Mel?" she called.

I stared up at Lassiter, trying to keep my voice low. "You're lucky we don't make you disappear right now!" I told him.

"Really?" Lassiter stepped closer to me. "Then why don't you? Why don't you do it?" His zombie breath was worse than the smell of the lizard tank at school.

I folded my arms. What was the answer? That we were bluffing?

"What is going on here?" Gramma demanded.

"It's nothing, Gramma," I said as I backed away from the zombie. "Nothing a quick spell won't fix." As I shuffled back, I noticed the way the soles of my high-tops slid over the floor. Sawdust! Mel kept fresh sawdust on the floor of the butcher shop. I bent down and picked up a handful.

"Let's see," I said quietly. "This should work just fine — for a spell to turn you into *dust*." I took a clump in my palm and blew sawdust toward the zombie. It flew right into the holes in his face, sticking to the gray ooze coming from his nose.

"Aargh!" Lassiter growled, swatting at the air. Suddenly, he didn't seem too sure whether my powers worked. He scrambled toward the door.

I brushed my hands together, relieved that he was leaving.

"You've fended me off for the moment." He swung his ax around and plunked it back into the crease along his spine. "But I'll be back. Till then, I trust you'll take good care of my slave."

"Get out!" I yelled, and Lassiter fumbled out the door.

I sucked in a breath. The zombie was gone. But I wasn't off the hook.

"Kyle!" Gramma snapped. "Shouting in a public place? You know better. And what's this about a spell?"

"It's . . . it's Tommy," I said, thinking fast. "We were doing a . . . a spelling bee outside, and he flubbed a word. We thought it would be nice to give him one more chance."

"Right," Amber said, turning toward a sign on the wall. "Okay, Tommy. Spell *cutlet.*"

Tommy's face came alive. *"Cutlet.* That's *K-U-T —*"

"Wrong!" Amber said as the butcher returned from the phone.

"Okay, what do we have here?" Mel picked up the two pieces of roast. "Which half do you want, then, Dinah?"

The butcher didn't miss a beat! I guess he thought he'd chopped it in half before the phone rang.

"We'll take the large portion," Gramma said.

She turned to Tommy. "All right, young man. Let's hear you spell *judgment*."

Tommy swallowed hard but started spelling. I had to hand it to him. He was learning fast. But so was Lassiter. He didn't seem to fear us anymore.

And that was going to be a problem.

# CHAPTER THIRTEEN

The spelling bee continued all over town. When Gramma wanted to see her friend Agnes at the diner, we spelled *entrée* and *menu* and *stroganoff*. We even tried *chrysanthemum* at the flower shop. That one knocked me out, but Zack eventually got it.

At last, Gramma finished her errands and loaded her sacks into the Cadillac's trunk. "You might as well pile in," she told us. "But fingers off the windows."

A few minutes later, we were cruising along inside the big car. I grinned. This thing was built like a tank. Definitely zombie-proof.

At home, we helped Gramma unload, then went out to the backyard.

"Where's your basketball?" Amber asked.

"In the garage." I turned back toward the house. "I'm going to bring out my Freaky Files and see what we can find."

While Amber and Zack shot some hoops, Tommy and I spread the Freaky Files out on the picnic table.

"I always wondered what was in this big old folder," Tommy said. "You used to carry it around school like it was a guidebook."

"Guidebook to the supernatural," I said, unclipping a stack of index cards. "So what do we do next? I think we need to stop Lassiter before he does more serious damage with that ax."

"Seriously," Tommy agreed. "He sliced that meat clean in half."

"I think the trial is a good idea," Amber said. "Did you tell them about the scarecrow movie? Maybe Lassiter can't move on until justice is done." She shot the ball. It rolled on the rim, then dropped through.

"I saw that movie!" Zack held the ball straight out, walking like a zombie. "Justice must be done! Scarecrow must have trial!"

Tommy watched, scratching his head. "So this is what you guys do on Saturdays? Zombie hunting?"

"You'll get used to it," I told him.

"I say we go for the trial," Zack said as he

dribbled the ball away from Amber. "A mock trial. We'll have a prosecutor, a judge, and even a defense attorney."

"I want to be the prosecutor," Tommy said. "I'll even wear a suit."

"I'm not sure you're ready," I said.

"Sure he is!" Amber came over to the table and sat across from Tommy. "You've got three major points to remember. One — he confessed to us. Two — there's the poem about his crime. And three — we have records from the sheriff's office. The sheriff found the stolen gold on Lassiter. And he wrote that there were two witnesses. Just make sure you include those points in the case."

Tommy nodded. "Got it . . . three points."

"Four," Zack said. "There's the ax in his back. Isn't that evidence of something? I guess it's proof that he was murdered."

"Okay, four points." Tommy held up four fingers. "Got it."

Amber pushed away from the table. "I'll be the judge. I'm a pretty fair person. And Zack can be the defense attorney."

"No way!" Zack passed the ball to Amber. "I'm up to my eyeballs in zombies. You seem to have forgotten Penelope is in my basement? I might not even be able to get away for the trials."

"You've got a zombie in your basement?" Tommy banged a fist on the table. "Cool! Is she tied up?"

"No," Zack said. "She was sleeping in the mud when I left." He looked at his watch. "I probably should get home. I hope she doesn't try to bake today."

"A zombie who cooks?" Tommy grinned. "This is better than I thought."

"Can we get back to the Files?" I asked Tommy. "You get the Monster Cards. I'll flip through my notes from horror classics."

"So Zack can be off the hook for the trial," Amber said. "That makes you the defense attorney, Kyle."

"Oh, right," I said. "I'm going to defend the man who's trying to kill my gramma."

"It's for a good cause," Amber said. "We're going to whop this bad dude straight off to the next dimension."

"Yeah, okay," I said, not liking the idea at all. "Somebody's got to do it."'

"So . . ." Tommy said, "when should we do it? I'll get Mom to iron my suit."

"That will depend on Lassiter," I said. "How are we going to get him to attend his own trial?"

"I guess a written invitation wouldn't do it?" Tommy asked. "A telegram? An e-mail?"

Amber and Zack laughed.

"No, wait," I said, pulling out a card from a movie about ant people. "I think Tommy's onto something. There's something like that in the files."

I read: "Freaky Files Entry: *Revenge of the Ant People* — tiny insect people throw a big picnic for their enemies. Once the enemies come, the ants surround them and turn the tables. One wild party."

"I love parties," Tommy said. "I'll bring the soda."

"We'll have to trick him," Zack said.

I nodded. "A trap."

Amber bounced the ball. "And the bait would be?"

"That's easy," Zack said. "Kyle's grand-mother."

"What?" I scowled at him. "No way."

"Why not? He's already following her around. We can use her to lure him to the trial."

"Uh-uh, no way." I folded my arms. "Too dangerous."

"Zack is right," Amber said. "Gramma's a natural. When is she going out again? Maybe we can string Lassiter along, have him follow her home. Then we could do the trial here."

I shook my head.

"Come on, Kyle," Tommy said. "Lassiter is going to haunt her anyway, right? So this way, there's an end in sight."

I sighed. "Okay, okay." I stared down at the Files, trying to think it out. "Tomorrow is the groundbreaking. I'll bet Lassiter will be there."

"Especially since the new school is being built over the zombies' old graves," Zack pointed out.

"That is probably the worst place for the trial." I straightened my tie, feeling like a special agent. We were coming up with a plan. "It's out of our control. And the other zombies might be around to help him."

"Like Dread," Amber said. "He sounds like bad news."

"So we wait until after the trial," Zack said, "when Gramma goes . . . where?"

"Back here," I said. "We're going to have brunch. Nothing special."

"Unless you invite one unexpected visitor,"

Amber said. "When Lassiter follows Gramma back, you need to let him in."

"And we'll be here," Tommy said. "Ready to prosecute."

I bit my lower lip. "Sounds messy."

Amber nodded. "Yeah, but what choice do we have?"

"All right." I flipped over the card for *Revenge of the Ant People*. "Now all I need is a major detour for the grown-ups. How am I going to get Gramma and the parents out of the house before Lassiter comes?"

That night as I pulled on a clean T-shirt, I wondered about our plan. Would it work?

If it was a success, Lassiter would be way gone by this time tomorrow. That thought made me sigh as I turned out the light and slid under the covers.

Lassiter would be gone. Gramma would be safe.

I closed my eyes, but something didn't feel right.

I sat up. I'd already checked on Gramma. She was fine. So why did I have goose bumps on my arms?

I went to the window. The backyard glowed with moonlight from the big saucer of a moon. An orange moon. Well, at least it wasn't red, like the zombie legend. Eerie light shone on the picnic table, the porch, the grass.

*Don't let yourself get spooked,* I thought. *We have a plan. A good one! Everything is going to be fine.*

My eyes traveled to the basketball hoop on the garage. The dark roof tiles seemed to be moving.

I squinted. No. Someone was sitting up there. Lassiter and Dread, on the roof of my garage.

"Oh, man!" I turned away, then looked back.

Lassiter was playing with his ax, a contented smile on his face. I couldn't see Dread's expression at all. What had Tommy called him? The grim reaper. There was a mystery about this zombie that bothered me. The guy was creepy.

Yawning, I pulled my desk chair over to the window. I sat down to keep watch for as long as I could stand it.

It was going to be a long night.

# CHAPTER FOURTEEN

I t feels weird being at the old cemetery during the day," I told my friends.

The ceremony was starting in ten minutes. We were walking on the hard-packed mud, along with about a hundred residents of Paxituckett.

Tommy wore a suit jacket that he thought made him look like a lawyer. Actually, he looked like his dad, who owns a car dealership — Arthur's Autos.

Amber was barely recognizable without her baseball cap. Her wild orange curls made her look . . . I don't know. Like a girl. I usually don't think of her that way.

Zack pulled at the collar of his shirt. "It always feels weird here. I don't know how we're going to go to school on top of this haunted ground."

"It's not haunted," Amber insisted. "Not anymore."

I pointed to the ridge of mud that I'd seen Sky sleeping in. "Tell that to the zombies who take their mud baths here." We were sure the zombies would show up today. The only question was when.

Ahead of us, Mom and Dad were walking with Gramma. Everyone was headed toward a blue-and-white-striped awning. Sort of like a tent in the desert. At the front of the awning was a podium, along with two big amplifiers. A few rows of folding chairs faced the stage area.

"Wow," Tommy said. "That sound system has enough amps to wake the dead."

"You said it, bro," I said, letting my shades fall onto my nose. I was feeling good about our plan. Okay, the zombies on the garage were a minor setback. But I woke up in one piece. And since Gramma spent the morning trying on different hats, I figured she was fine, too.

So far, so good.

I looked ahead. Gramma stood out in her green print dress and green wide-brimmed hat. In this freaky landscape of dirt on dirt, any splash of color stood out. Mom wore a gold blazer, but Dad was completely lost in brown.

"Okay," I said. "Gramma is giving a speech. Looks like she's got a seat under the awning."

"We should probably split up for better security," Zack said.

"Right." I snapped my fingers. "We can have one person at each corner of the perimeter."

"Perimeter?" Tommy scrunched up his face. "What is this, geometry class?"

"You need to stay with your parents, Kyle," Amber said to me.

"Right." I scoped out the area around the awning. "Looks like Mom and Dad are in the reserved seats. Okay. Then I'll stick with them, close to Gramma."

"I'll head over to the right front," Zack said. "That way we've got the stage covered."

"Tommy and I will go to the back." Amber shielded her eyes from the sun. "But it's going to be hard to see over all these people."

I pointed to the tree Zack and I had used for our stakeout. "Why don't you climb up there?"

Zack nodded. "It worked for us. We were hiding up there the other night. Until Tommy came."

Tommy and Amber sized up the tree.

"That might work," she said.

"Yeah, right." Tommy scratched the back of his neck. "Like I'm going to climb up there."

"We'll give you a boost," I said. "Once you reach that first branch, it's easy."

Tommy shook his head. "I don't think so. I'm not so light on my feet. I like the ground."

"I'll climb the tree and be the lookout," Amber said. "Tommy can be my legs on the ground."

Tommy nodded. "Works for me."

"Okay, keep your eyes open," I said as a group of teachers from our school moved ahead to take their seats.

I ducked my head, hoping Ms. Witker wouldn't drop by and correct my grammar. There's something weird about seeing teachers outside of school. You know they have a life beyond the chalkboard. But you don't want to go there.

"Watch out for the special guests." Zack said as he headed off. "Of the *undead* persuasion."

I walked up to the first aisle, where my parents were talking with our school principal, Mr. Gill. Big gulp. Not that I get in trouble at school, but I try to keep a low profile. And that's not easy when you're chasing a zombie down the halls.

"Good morning, Kyle," Mr. Gill said. "I'll bet you're quite proud of your grandmother today."

"Definitely," I said, looking over at Gramma. A wide smile lit her face as a photographer snapped a photo of her with the mayor. Just beyond them, Hayley Frazier waited near the podium in a fancy dress and white gloves. I guessed she'd been chosen to help out with the ceremony. She smiled at me.

I smiled back. Then I turned away, feeling like a goon. Did I have to smile so big?

The seats were quickly filling up.

"Looks like they're getting ready to start," Dad said. "You'll want to be up there with the VIPs, Mr. Gill."

"Indeed." The principal shook Dad's hand, then joined the group under the awning.

The mayor opened the ceremony, welcoming everyone. He talked about the value of education, and I sort of tuned out. Where was Lassiter? I turned to scan the crowd behind me.

"Be still!" Mom murmured.

I turned back, not wanting to meet her eyes. She didn't understand the danger.

Next, Gramma was introduced. I clapped extra hard.

"Mayor Malkowitz has talked about gratitude

toward your teachers," Gramma began. "Well, I'm here today to share with you my personal thanks for letting me be a part of the lives of children. It's given me a world of joy."

Gramma was still talking when I spotted them — the zombies.

Dread floated to front and center, right up to Gramma. He lingered there, like her shadow. The urge to rush up to her and nudge him away tore at me, but I couldn't jump into Gramma's speech. Not when Dread wasn't doing anything to hurt her.

Meanwhile, Lassiter and the guy in the lab coat were edging up to the side of the awning. So far, no sign of Sky. I wondered if she was still sleeping.

I wasn't sure what to do. Since none of the adults could see them, I couldn't step up and order them to leave. At the end of the line, Hayley leaned forward to stare. I knew she could see the zombies. What was she thinking? What if she said something?

I glanced over at Zack. He shrugged, sort of saying, *What now?* I wasn't sure.

The zombies stood off to the side as Gramma finished her speech.

Everyone applauded. I checked the zombies as I clapped. They were milling around. And Lassiter was pointing up.

Now the VIPs stood in a line, with Gramma on the front end. Hayley Frazier passed down the line, handing each person a bouquet. When she reached Dread, she paused and frowned. Her expression was clear. She knew he didn't belong with the VIPs. *He doesn't even belong in this century,* I thought. Finally, Hayley stepped around him and handed the last bouquet to Gramma.

So far so good. But what were the zombies up to?

As I watched, the zombie in the lab coat gave Lassiter a boost. He pushed him up, so that Lassiter could reach the top of the awning, over the speakers.

What were they trying to do? I knew that the awning could never hold Lassiter's weight.

And he seemed to know that. He didn't climb to the top, which I couldn't even see from down here. He just . . . kept reaching.

That was when my cell phone started ringing.

Mom glared at me as I reached in my pocket.

My parents had given me the cell as a way to keep in touch. But I had strict warnings to keep it turned off in school and church. I turned away from Mom. I knew I was going to hear about this later.

I flipped the phone open and pressed it to my ear. "What?" I whispered.

"It's me . . . Tommy." Typical Tommy Hernandez. Calling me on my cell in the middle of something important. He probably had a lame-o joke to tell me.

I winced. "I can't talk now!"

"Amber told me to call you," Tommy said. "There's a shovel on that tent thingie."

"What?"

"There's a shovel — a big one — sitting on the awning," Tommy said breathlessly. "Lassiter is pushing it. Sliding it down."

I looked ahead of me. Suddenly, it was so obvious.

Gramma stood at the end of the line of VIPs. Just on this side of the awning. If that shovel slid down, it was going to land right on her head!

# CHAPTER FIFTEEN

I looked from Lassiter to the awning.

I couldn't see the shovel. No way to tell if it was about to fall. But I couldn't stand there and let it happen.

I sprang forward, into Gramma's arms.

"Kyle!" Her eyes grew wide with surprise. "What the devil —"

I just put my head down and pushed like a ram.

Gramma took a few steps back and knocked into our principal.

Mr. Gill seemed equally surprised.

There was a slight gasp from the audience. Then the shovel shot down. It dropped from the awning and clanged onto the ground. It banged right onto Gramma's footprints.

"Oh, my!" Gramma blinked.

"What a terrible accident," the principal said.

"Who left that there?" the mayor asked, stepping around to look up at the awning. "Someone could have been hurt."

"Fortunately, Kyle saw it coming." Gramma put her arms around me. "Glad to see you were awake, child."

Hayley gaped at me, totally impressed.

Okay, I admit it. I got a big charge out of that.

The mayor spoke into the microphone. "Well, ladies and gentlemen, it seems that fate has pushed our groundbreaking ahead of schedule," he said. "It's not often that we see a shovel fall from the sky."

The audience chuckled.

"Fortunately, no one was harmed. Let's proceed with our program."

As the mayor went on, I turned to check on Lassiter and the other zombie.

They were gone.

I shot a look at Zack. He pointed to the rear of the crowd. Then I spotted the two zombies marching toward the back. As the speeches went on, they went to the center aisle of chairs and stood there, watching.

What were they going to try next?

I didn't want to take any chances. I stayed at Gramma's side.

"You were great!" Amber said, smacking my back after the ceremony.

"Thanks to your tip," I said, looking from Amber to Tommy. "I couldn't see that shovel at all."

"No one up front could see it," Tommy said.

"That was the beauty of my lookout spot." Amber nodded over my shoulder. "There's Zack. How are we going to get the next part of our plan going?"

Zack joined us. "So far so good, but two zombies at six o'clock."

"Are you going to invite them over?" Tommy asked me.

That had been the plan. But now, watching Lassiter, I worried that it wouldn't work. "He'll smell a trap," I said. "I need to try something else."

"Well, think fast," Zack said anxiously.

We all turned as Lassiter approached us. His bloodshot eye was trained on me, as if I were his target. I felt my stomach twist. He was one creepy dead man.

"You consider yourself clever?" he sputtered at me.

I leaned back. Whenever he opened his mouth, the guy was all tooth rot. Don't want to go there.

"Kyle *is* clever," Amber said. "He saved his gramma."

"Face it, Lassiter," I said. "You've lost."

"Ha! We will not lose. I have promised Dread I will bring him a slave, and that I will do!"

I mulled that over, wondering why Dread was so important in this whole slave deal.

I wasn't sure about that yet, but I *could* tell that Lassiter wanted to impress the cloaked zombie. I decided to issue a challenge. "How many times have you flubbed it?" I asked the zombie. "Face it, man, you'll never get my gramma. From here on, the only way you could get close to her would be at . . . at my house."

"That's right," Zack said, with a slow smile. He'd picked up on my strategy. "But you can't get into Kyle's house. Not with the lock on the door."

"Bolts and chains shall not stop me!" Lassiter insisted. "I shall push the door in!"

"Never happen." Amber waved him off. "You're too scared. You know we have *the spell*!"

"Do you think I fear you?" Lassiter rasped. "You are no match for my strength . . . my cunning." His eye glowed red. He wasn't going to back down.

*Perfect!* I thought. But I stayed cool.

I shrugged. "Whatever." Then we turned away and walked back toward the street.

"Do you think he'll go for it?" Tommy whispered.

"Definitely," Amber said. "He snapped up that bait like a hungry piranha."

"Lassiter will be there as soon as he can zombie-walk over," Zack said. "Now we just have to get the adults out of your house."

"I've got an idea for that," I said. "We'll meet back at my house. Soon as you can. But don't ring the bell. Hang in the backyard until you see my parents leave."

"What if they won't go?" Tommy's face was pinched with worry.

"Don't even go there," I said, heading to where the Cadillac was parked.

My parents were already standing by Gramma's car. Dad motioned to me. "Let's go, Kyle."

"Later," I said to my friends. I walked over to

the car, thinking about our plan. If it went off without a hitch, I'd be shocked. I'd learned that zombies didn't like to follow orders. Parents were even worse.

Sitting in the backseat with Mom, I crossed my fingers. We needed all the luck we could get.

# CHAPTER SIXTEEN

O nce we were home, I stepped into the kitchen to start stage two of my plan. Gramma was setting up the coffeemaker. Mom was slicing melon. Dad sat at the table, reading the newspaper.

"I almost forgot!" I smacked my forehead — good for effect. "I talked to Agnes from the diner. She wanted you to stop by and see her."

"What?" Gramma put two mugs on the counter. "When did she call?"

The truth was, I had called Agnes. "I talked to her this morning. Anyway, she said she was making a fresh batch of sticky buns. Dad's favorite."

Dad lowered his newspaper. "I didn't hear the phone ring this morning."

"You were in the shower or something," I said. "But Agnes was hoping she could celebrate with you, Gramma. With all of us." I watched as Mom and Dad exchanged a look. "Hey, why don't you guys go now?"

"I guess we could do that." Dad folded up the paper.

"We'll have our family celebration afterward," Mom said. She wiped her hands on the dish towel.

Gramma took her big green hat from the table and stepped into the hallway. "Come on, Kyle," she said, adjusting her hat in the mirror she had given us.

"Actually, I was planning to hang here," I said.

Mom frowned. "Why don't you come with us, sugar?"

I hate it when she calls me that. "I have some homework to do," I said. "And my friends will be here soon."

"With no adults in the house?" Mom rubbed her hands together. It was as if she could smell something in the air. Mothers have that weird sixth sense. They know when you're just *thinking* about breaking the rules. "Maybe I should stay."

"Ma! I can handle being home alone. I do it almost every day after school."

She touched my shoulder. "I know, Kyle, but —"

"Give the boy some space, Carol," Dad told her. Lucky for me, he didn't have that parental radar thing going on. "He'll be okay, and we won't be long."

Gramma paused at the side door. "No wild parties while we're gone," she said. Then she smiled, like it was a huge joke.

"We'll keep it under control, Gramma," I said. No parties. Just a zombie-fest.

Peering over the kitchen curtains, I watched as Gramma's Cadillac pulled out of the driveway. One more part of the plan in place. Now I just needed to lure Lassiter into the house for a trial. He would be here in a few minutes. That was, if he didn't run into Gramma and follow her to the diner.

I cracked open the kitchen door. Where were my fellow squad members? If Tommy's dad dropped them off, they would have been here by now.

No one in sight. I walked out to the back porch. The yard was quiet and still. Then I heard a sneeze. It seemed to come from the fence. No . . . the bushes.

"You're standing on my feet." That was Amber's voice.

"I can't help it," said Tommy. "Zack's got his head up my armpit."

"That's your armpit?" Zack exploded out of the hedges. "*Blech*!"

Amber and Tommy followed him.

"Nice hiding place," I said. "I'll have to remember it next time Mom wants me to clean the basement."

Amber opened her mouth and plucked out a leaf. "It was Zack's idea. I wanted to circle the block one more time, but he said no."

"I didn't want Lassiter to see us," Zack said as he climbed onto the porch. "I was afraid he'd get suspicious."

"Good point," I said, waving them up from the yard. "Let's go in before he shows up."

Once inside, I ran upstairs to get my Freaky Files. I set the big blue folder on the kitchen table beside a box of doughnuts. Tommy had already helped himself.

"We can have the trial in here," I said.

"Works for me," Tommy said, sucking sugar off his thumb.

Zack opened up his backpack. "Bring any Cheez Whiz?" I asked.

He shook his head and pulled out a tangle

of rope. "I brought the rope you asked for. And here's the copy of the records from the sheriff's office. I thought we might need it for the trial."

Tommy nodded as Zack put the papers on the table. "That's for one of my four points," Tommy said. When I blinked in surprise, he added, "See? I remember." He pressed a finger to his forehead, smudging powered sugar there.

"And here's another point," I said, pulling a book out from under my Files. "'The Ballad of Lassiter.' So I guess we're set."

"Right. Now all we need is the guest of honor." Amber peeked into the bread drawer. "Got any chips?"

I went in the pantry to check. On the way, I passed the side door and almost choked on my tongue.

Lassiter's mealy face was pressed against the glass. His gooey closed eye looked like a jellyfish smooshed on the window. I reminded myself to get the Windex out after this thing was over.

"Grrr!" He rattled the door in its hinges. He was going to rip it off.

"It's open!" I cried. The last thing I needed

was for my parents to come home and find the storm door dangling from its hinges.

The kitchen was silent as he pulled the door open and stomped in.

"Where is she?" he growled. "Where is the smart one . . . the old and wise one who shall be our slave?"

"She . . . she's upstairs," I said, flustered. How was this part supposed to go? How were we going to get him to sit still during his trial?

Amber stepped forward. "She'll be down in a minute," she told the zombie. "Why don't you have a seat?"

"Sure," Zack said. "Sit down, have a doughnut. Or Kyle will fry you up some eggs or brains or something."

*Don't tick him off,* I thought as I edged toward the counter. Zack had left the rope there. The rope we planned to use to tie Lassiter in place.

I moved slowly. The zombie didn't seem to care. I reached to the side. My hands were on it. My hands were closing around it. On the count of three, I would swipe it off the counter and tie it around Lassiter like a lasso.

One . . . two . . .

I grabbed the rope, and something scuttled to the floor at my feet.

I looked down. Plastic handles of jump ropes.

"Jump ropes?" I asked Zack.

He shrugged. "Where's a kid supposed to get rope?"

Lassiter swung around to gape at us. "How could such a wise woman have such a foolish grandson?"

I was too busy trying to fling the rope around Lassiter to answer. I tried to toss it around him without touching him, but it flopped onto the floor. The other end knocked into the box of doughnuts, sending powered sugar flying.

Lassiter stepped toward me. His dirty boot stomped on the limp rope. "This is no time for games." He reached out, and I felt his fingers stab at my chest. Bony points sank into my shirt. "Get her for me. Now."

My heart thudded in my chest. Could he feel it hammering like crazy? I realized he was holding me off the floor. My heels barely touched the ground.

"I told you, she's upstairs," I said, trying to stay calm. Okay, the rope didn't work. Time for

Plan B. Which would be awesome — if we had a Plan B.

He growled and swung me toward the hallway.

"I don't think that was the answer he wanted," Tommy said nervously from behind me.

"Upstairs?" the zombie said. "Fine, then. We shall fetch her." He dragged me across the kitchen floor, into the hall. I felt helpless, dangling like a puppet.

This was not going well. But if I didn't stop him now, it would only get worse.

"Put me down," I said. "She's not upstairs."

"What's that you say?" His eye bulged curiously.

"She isn't there. I was lying."

He dropped me and my high-tops hit the floor. I stood face-to-face with the zombie. The very ticked-off zombie.

"You lied to me?" he rasped.

"Because I had to stop you," I said. "Someone has to stop you, Lassiter. And that's why we're here. It's time that you faced the wrong you did in your life."

"Hogwash," he murmured. "Stand clear of my path."

"No!" I stood my ground. Okay, maybe not the brightest move. But if I could stall him for a minute, maybe Zack and Amber could get those ropes around him from behind.

Or, if he got so mad that he put a whammy on me, maybe, just maybe . . . I stepped back, realizing our new mirror was just behind me on the wall. The mirror. If Great-Gramma Felicia could see her mirror now, she'd be fanning herself like crazy.

The frame pressed into my back. My secret weapon.

I swung around. "You're not getting past me," I said, baiting the zombie.

That did it. Lassiter lifted his hand and pointed his splayed fingers at my face. From the fierce light in his eye, I knew this wasn't good. He would get me out of his way, all right.

He was putting a whammy on me.

One more second, and I was going to be frozen stiff.

# CHAPTER SEVENTEEN

Everything I had learned about the whammy rushed through my head. I knew there was no way out, no way to fight it.

But I did have an idea.

I ducked.

Just as Lassiter shot the evil look at me, I fell to the floor.

That left him standing in the hall, staring into the gold-framed mirror. Staring at his own reflection.

Putting the whammy on himself.

From my crouch, I saw my friends eyeing me with a weird mixture of horror and admiration. No one knew if this would work, but it was worth a try.

"What's happening?" Still on the floor, I scuttled away from the zombie. My head banged into Zack's knees.

"I think it worked!" Amber stepped up to Lassiter and waved a hand in front of his face.

The zombie didn't move. His hand was frozen in the air, his crooked fingers pointing into the mirror.

"Woo-hoo! He put a whammy on himself!" Zack said, rubbing his hands together. "Boy, are you lucky that mirror was there."

"Luck? I don't think so." I stood up and dusted off my pants. "I planned it that way."

"You did?" Amber's eyes were bright. "When did you plan that move?"

"About . . . ten seconds ago," I admitted, "but it worked, right?"

Tommy was leaning close to Lassiter, testing him. He flicked the zombie's cheek. No reaction.

"Easy, Tommy," Zack said. "We want him to stay that way."

"Is that the same spell he put on me?" Tommy asked.

"Yeah," I answered, "and it's going to wear off. We need to start the trial."

"Right." Tommy cracked his knuckles.

"Okay!" Amber scratched her curls into a frenzy. "If I'm the judge, I'd better get this going." She hopped onto the kitchen counter and folded her arms, trying to look like a judge.

"Hold on," I said, digging through the junk

drawer for a crab mallet. I untangled the wooden hammer from a tangle of rubber bands and handed it to Amber.

"Cool." She slammed it on the counter. "Court is now in session. This man, Isaac Lassiter, is accused of killing a man named Nathan Fuller," Amber announced. "Oh, and apparently, he also stole Nathan's sack of gold." She turned to Tommy. "Mr. Prosecutor? Present your case."

Tommy paced. "Four points, four points," he repeated nervously. "Okay. Here's my case. Number one — you've got an ax in your back. Which leads me to believe that you really cheesed somebody off."

"Objection!" I said.

My friends stared at me.

"Objection?" Zack gasped. "What is this, *Law and Order*?"

"But that's sort of a stretch," I said. "I mean, is my client going to be held responsible for having an ax in his back?"

"Good point." Amber banged the gavel. "Not his fault. Go on, Tommy."

"Okay . . . four points." Tommy counted off one finger then nodded. "Number two is the poem written about you." He waggled the library book before the zombie's dazed eye. "I won't bother to read it all out loud again. Everyone here heard it yesterday. But it's evidence."

"Okay, wait," I said. "We don't have time to read it, but you need to say what it's about."

"Are you crazy?" Zack gaped at me. "He's going to come out of the whammy."

"I'm trying to make this like a real trial," I said. "But hurry."

Tommy opened the book, pressing one hand to his head. "What do I read?"

"Just give us the main points," Judge Amber said.

"Okay, okay." Tommy ran his finger down the page. "It says . . . well, mostly that Lassiter killed that man, Nathan Fuller, to get his gold."

Amber nodded. "We'll accept the poem as evidence."

"Yes!" Tommy shot his fist in the air and did a little dance. With a big guy like Tommy, a little dance takes some space.

Very slowly, Lassiter lifted his head to watch Tommy. That was when I realized the whammy was starting to fade.

"Zombie waking up. Let's move!" I shouted.

"Right!" Tommy stepped back to the table. "Point three, the records from the sheriff's office. Where the heck are they?"

I dug through my Freaky Files until I found the copies.

"Thanks. This is three," Tommy said, handing them to Amber. "The sheriff says that the defendant was found with the stolen gold in his possession." Tommy grinned. "Dang, I sound good. Anyway, Lassiter had the gold, and there were also two witnesses." He stood up and pointed a finger at Lassiter. "Two witnesses who *saw* this man commit murder!"

Judge Amber was nodding. I had to admit, Tommy was getting into this.

"Okay, one more point. Number four . . ." He swung back to Lassiter, scowling at him. "The nail in your coffin, buddy. Your confession."

"Objection," I said. "Hearsay?" Okay, it was lame, but I had to at least try to do my job. Besides, they said that all the time on Dad's favorite TV shows.

"He confessed in front of all of us." Judge Amber scratched her head under her baseball cap. "Sorry, counselor," she told me, "but in my book, that's proof that he's guilty. This dude did the dirty deed."

Tommy's fist shot into the air again. "Thank you, Judge Judy!"

"Wait!" I said, holding up my hands. "My client is coming out of the whammy. Maybe he wants to defend himself."

Tommy stopped his happy dance.

"Like he's going to tell the truth now?" Zack said, raking a hand over his short hair.

Amber shrugged. "I don't trust him, but okay."

I edged close to the zombie, trying to ignore the rotting holes in his skin. "This is your chance," I told him. "If you didn't kill Nathan Fuller, speak now."

His one eye rolled toward me. The stern expression on his face softened. It turned into a sneer.

"I killed him," he said slowly. "Indeed, I did. And proud of it, I am."

I swallowed hard, realizing that I was staring into the face of evil.

The other zombies had rotting skin and moldy teeth. But Lassiter was different. He was rotten through and through. I stepped back, shivering.

"I wanted those riches," the zombie went on. "The gold Nathan bragged about. So I took it all. And I didn't mind that I had to kill him to get it."

I glanced over at my friends. Tommy wasn't dancing anymore. Zack's eyes were wide with horror.

Amber nervously chewed her lower lip. "Oh, dude," she said sadly, "you are *so* guilty."

Lassiter snapped his head toward her. "Indeed." His black-pocked teeth gleamed as he grinned. "Guilty and proud of it."

Judge Amber slammed the mallet on the table. "That's the final verdict — guilty as charged." She folded her arms and looked at me. "Okay, Agent K. How do we make sure this guy pays for his crime?"

"What can you do to me?" Lassiter sniped. "I'm already dead."

But then the air began to swirl around him. A weird light swelled over the zombie.

"He's transforming!" I said. "It worked!"

"We did it!" Amber clapped her hands together. "The trial was what he needed."

165

"Cool!" Tommy said.

Lassiter straightened within the cocoon of light. It was as if he was being lifted by an invisible force. But the scowl on his face didn't soften. And this time, the light was not golden, as we'd seen with the other zombies.

It was dark red. Crimson.

It made us all shrink back.

"What's happening?" Zack asked frantically.

My heart started thudding in my chest. Had we done something wrong?

We had expected Lassiter to be transformed into his handsome, healthy self. The way he looked when he was alive. That's what had happened with the other zombies when we solved their key issues.

But inside the red light, Lassiter was rotting even more. Rotting to the core.

"What's going on?" I said, staring at the decomposing figure at the center of the red light. "This is all wrong!"

# CHAPTER EIGHTEEN

**N**o!" he cried. "You cast the spell upon me! How did you do it? I will not disappear!"

The skin seemed to melt from his bones. The bones turned to dust. The dust dropped down into a pile of ash on the hall rug.

"What is that about?" Amber asked.

We edged closer, cautiously, staring down at the ashes in horror.

Zack's face was pale. "This is creeping me out."

"Something went wrong," I said. "Or . . . something is different here."

A dark crimson shadow rose up from the pile of dust.

It was Lassiter. We all knew it.

Then, before our eyes, a big black box appeared. A coffin . . . or maybe a vault? The lid creaked open, and it seemed to be pulling Lassiter's ghost inside it.

The crimson ghost started swirling into the box.

"No!" Lassiter's voice echoed. "I will undo your magic!" he threatened. "I will return!" His voice was sucked into the box, along with his red shadow.

And then — *clunk!* The vault closed.

We were all quiet for a minute. Dumbstruck. Then — "Cool," Tommy said.

And suddenly, it was just the four of us standing in my hall. The dust was gone from the carpet. The air was clear of crimson clouds and echoing zombie voices.

"At least he took his ashes with him," Zack pointed out.

"Probably the nicest thing Lassiter ever did for us," Amber said.

I nodded. "My mom would have pitched a fit. She got this rug over in Japan or something."

I turned toward the mirror with the gold frame. Gramma's gift had saved my skin. I smiled at my own reflection. Maybe the mirror possessed some magic.

Naah . . . .

A half hour later, you would never know we'd just watched a zombie meltdown in my house.

"Let's play another game," Amber said,

bouncing the basketball in the driveway. "Low scorer gets to go back to the graveyard and cheese Dread again."

"Don't even think about it," I said, picking up a rebound and taking a shot. It bounced off the rim. "Pretty soon, Dread is going to figure a way around our snack attacks."

Zack caught the ball and started dribbling. "Don't ever underestimate the power of cheese," he said.

"Really," Tommy called from the picnic table. "Dairy rules." He sat there, slurping down a yogurt stick. Tommy had tried to raid the fridge, but yogurt was the best we could do.

"Let's take a break," I said. I swiped at the ball, trying to steal it from Amber. She passed it behind her back to Zack. "I want to update the Freaky Files."

I stretched my arms up toward the sky and took a deep, cool breath. Lassiter was gone, and Gramma was safe. Mission accomplished.

"Oh, man!" I put my hands on my head as a thought hit me. "Do you think Dread will go after Gramma now?"

"Not if she leaves for Florida tomorrow," Zack said. "I mean, I can't see Dread following her there. Though he might keep looking for the human slave. The one mentioned in the legend."

"For some reason," I said, opening my giant blue notebook, "Paxituckett seems to be a zombie magnet now. Dread isn't even from this area, right? Wasn't he one of the zombies who came on the train?"

Amber nodded. "Yup." She sat at the table and hugged the basketball. "What do you think it is about this place? Is Paxituckett a corridor to another world or something?"

I grinned. "Aw, man, there are a million possibilities on that one." I flipped to a clean page. "Time to start up a new file. It could be a magnetic field here. Or a magic stone in the old graveyard."

Tommy was hanging on my every word. "This is so cool!" His cheeks dimpled as he smiled. "Zombie hunters!"

"And we just completed yet another successful mission," I said, feeling a swell of pride. "Another zombie gone."

"But to where?" Zack asked. "Lassiter didn't turn gold and head off to La La Land like the others."

Zack was right. Lassiter didn't have a happy

ending. "Do you think he went . . . ?" I pointed down, my voice trailing off.

"Creepy!" Amber shuddered. "I don't even want to think about it!"

"And he said he'd be back," Zack pointed out. "Do you think he can do that?"

"No way!" Tommy insisted. "He's just a sore loser."

I looked toward the house, scene of the zombie's last stand. "Let's hope he was just bragging," I said. "This is definitely something new for the Freaky Files." I went back into the kitchen and sat at the table. "New Entry. What should I call it? When bad zombies transform?"

"Zombie meltdown," Tommy suggested. "That's what it looked like, his skin melting off his bones." He squirted some cherry yogurt on his arm, then licked it off.

"Tommy," Amber said. "If you are going to hang out with us, you are going to have to clean up your act a little."

Tommy smirked. But at least he didn't argue.

"You know, it might make sense," Zack said. "If you think about it, Lassiter doesn't belong in the land of golden light, with Chastity and Jeremiah. He was bad to the end. Bad to the bone."

"And he never felt bad about what he did," Amber said. "Creepazoid."

I started writing on an index card. Freaky Files Entry: Bad to the Bone Zombie.

"I gotta hand it to you, Kyle," Zack told me. "You've made some awesome moves in the past few days. I never thought we'd get rid of Lassiter."

"Yeah." I sat back and touched my tie. "We did it, man!"

"You know, Kyle," Zack clapped a hand on my shoulder. "You should be president of the Zombie Squad."

"No way, man!" I laughed. "You're the one who found them!"

Zack shook his head. "I never wanted it to happen!"

"Wait, wait!" Tommy gaped. "You mean, there's a club? This is so cool! Can I be vice president?"

"Sure," Amber said.

"You can be anything you want," I said. "President, VP, or Agent T. We're that flexible."

"Yeah . . ." Zack's face lit up as he hit on an idea. "And I know just what your first official duty should be. There's a zombie in my base-ment —"

"Who really needs someone to keep an eye on her," I interrupted.

"Oh, right!" Amber said. "Penelope. She loves to bake."

"Really? That's perfect!" Tommy's dimples were back. "Because I *love* cookies!"